The Piper

Rebel Hearts, Volume 2

Lily Baldwin

Published by Lily Baldwin, 2021.

THE PIPER

First edition. November 18, 2021.

Written by Lily Baldwin.

For anyone who needs to hear the words... *You are enough*.

Chapter One

Lady Cait Campbell stood on a stool while Helen, her maid, knelt on the floor, pinning the hem of Cait's new tunic.

"This shade of plum is so becoming on ye, my lady," Helen said brightly as she paused to tuck a wayward lock of her own flaxen hair back into the knot piled on top of her head.

Cait felt her cheeks burn. "I'm certain 'tis not."

Helen cocked a brow at Cait. "One of these days, I'm going to pay ye a compliment, and ye're not going to protest or blush." Helen straightened her back and puffed out her chest. "Ye're going to stand proud and simply say, thank ye, Helen."

A pang of guilt struck Cait's heart. "I did not mean to appear ungrateful. I'm sorry. I—"

"Hush, pet," Helen crooned. The stern set to her features softened as she stood, folding the Lady of Castle Shéan in her arms. "Ye didn't do anything wrong. I was just trying to encourage ye to...to..." The maid's words trailed off as she sighed. "I don't ken what I was trying to do." Helen lifted her shoulders. "All I ken is that I'm standing in the presence of the most beautiful, talented, and kindest lady in the Highlands, and no one would seek to contradict me on this point...except for ye." Helen's warm green eyes sought Cait's gaze.

Cait took a deep breath as she forced an impassive expression on her face all the while her stomach twisted, and fear made her chest ache. "I'm just...I'm nervous about..." She swallowed hard. "Yuletide is upon us..." Her knees felt like they were about to give out. "Please," she said, reaching for Helen's hand. "I must sit."

"My lady, ye're trembling!" Helen led Cait to a chair by the hearth. "Ye've gotten yerself in a right state, I can tell. And all my talk has not helped, I'd wager."

Nothing helped. Everything hurt.

Cait could hardly draw breath. "I...I just don't see why I need a new tunic."

Helen chuckled softly. "Bless ye, my lady. Is that all this is about? Yer father is a generous man as are yer brothers. They have no other lady to spoil but ye."

Cait held out the billowing sleeves of the costly Flemish wool she wore. "This is no simple garb. It might be something a bride would wear."

Helen sat down in the chair next to Cait and reached out, gently clasping her hands. "Look me in the eyes, my lady, and hear my words. They're not intending to marry ye off. Ye ken that yer family would never do that. They just want ye to have something especially lovely to wear for the upcoming festivities."

Cait's stomach dropped out. "I knew it." She clenched and unclenched her fists against the sensation that her fingers were going numb. "They want me to attend the feasts."

Helen's brows drew together. "Of course, they do, my lady. 'Tis Yule, after all."

Cait shot Helen a knowing look. "Do not pretend like ye don't know why I'm upset."

Helen shrugged with false casualness. "It won't be as bad as ye think."

Cait closed her eyes, trying to calm her racing heart. "Ye're probably right," she said weakly, although she knew Helen was mistaken.

A knock sounded at the door.

Cait stiffened.

Helen held out a soothing hand. "Ye're all right, my lady. Just breathe."

Incapable of breathing, Cait sat frozen while Helen crossed the room and opened the door. Her eldest brother entered the room.

Normally, when Matthew came to her chamber to visit with her, she was elated, but she knew this was not one of their usual visits.

Matthew's thick, curly black hair was pulled away from his handsome face, which shone with pride as he walked toward her. "Cait, ye're a vision!"

She managed to smile despite the knot of tears lodged in her throat, but judging by the way her brother's smile vanished, she knew she had failed to hide her trepidation.

"Kindly leave us, Helen," he said quietly to her maid.

Helen dipped in a quick curtsy, then hastened from the room; meanwhile, Matthew crossed to her side and claimed the chair next to hers. On another night, Cait would have giggled, watching her brother with his mighty shoulders, thick neck, and muscular thighs perch on the delicate high-backed chair near her hearth, but at that moment, she couldn't muster a spark of gaiety.

He leaned forward and covered her hands with his strong, calloused fingers. "Cait, have I ever put ye in harm's way?"

She met his silver gaze and shook her head.

"Laird Ewan MacLeod is a fine man, as is his mother and brother. Ye needn't fear them."

She shifted her gaze to the dancing flames, crackling in the hearth bed. "I do not fear them. I ken they mean me no harm. I just...I'm not comfortable meeting new people. And ye ken gatherings make me nervous—all those people, the din. Why can we just not celebrate as a family like we do every year?"

"Ewan is not a stranger to ye."

She raised a brow at her brother. "Matthew, I was eight when last he visited."

Matthew smiled, revealing the gap between his two front teeth. "Och, what a precocious lass ye were then, and how ye doted on Ewan. He was ten and five, and quick to laugh and make merry in those days." A distant look came into her brother's eyes as he chuckled softly. "I remember a Sabbath that was particularly stormy. Ye were frightened by the rumble of thunder. None of us could comfort ye but Ewan. He bundled ye up in his arms and rocked ye in a chair by the fire. He told ye stories, and ye sang together and laughed. Don't ye remember?"

Memories of a young man with golden hair and bright, cheerful eyes flashed in her mind. "I do," she said, lifting her shoulders. "But I am one and twenty now." She swallowed the knot of tears in her throat. "I'm not that precocious lass anymore."

Matthew looked her straight on. "Cait, ye can do this. I know ye can. Consider last spring when ye traveled with us all the way to Brodie territory and spent several days amidst a new clan."

"That was different," she said, crossing her arms over her chest. "I did that for Nathan so that our brother could see me in the flesh and know that I was alive after he believed me dead for so many years."

Matthew raked his hand through his hair. "I ken it was different."

"Nathan blamed himself for what happened to me," Cait added. "Father blamed him, too, at least in the beginning. 'Tis why I had to go—to help set things right between them. I would do anything for my family, even face my greatest fears." The mention of facing her fears made her heart beat faster. She could feel her panic grow, but she was careful not to show it.

Matthew sat back and expelled a slow breath. Cait could feel his mounting frustration. An instant later, he stood and took her hands and pulled her to her feet. "Look around ye, Cait." His voice held a note of urgency.

She did as he bade her. Her gaze settled on her four-poster bed with its blue quilt, dotted with white embroidered flowers. Then she scanned her walls, which were covered in tapestries made by her own hand. In that moment, a quiet delight entered her heart. The tapestries were vibrant with intricate patterns that told stories—some of which were true and heartbreaking, while others were forged within her own imagination and told of the woman she might have been if only she were stronger. Then her gaze settled on her bedside table where her pipe lay. It was her greatest treasure. When she played, her mind quieted, giving her soul reprieve from haunting memories that she otherwise couldn't escape.

"These walls are real," Matthew said, drawing her gaze as he placed his hand on the stones above the mantle. "Our keep is built on solid ground. Yer father is strong." He placed his hand on his heart. "As are yer brothers. We will never let harm befall ye again." He crossed to her side.

She swallowed hard. "I ken."

He knelt in front of her. "I ken ye know that. But knowing something and believing something are two different things. Ye must believe, Cait!"

She cast her gaze to the ground. "I know," she muttered. "I...I will try." The distant echo of screams came slowly to the fore of her mind, growing louder with every second, mocking her, proving to her that she would never forget. Tears stung her eyes.

"Look at me," Matthew beseeched her, his silver eyes pleading. "Seven years have passed since the ferry boat overturned and we thought we lost ye forever. But ye're safe now, Cait—safe and so dearly loved."

Despite how she tried to hold them back, her tears pushed past the confines of her lids. "I know."

Matthew pulled her close. "Believe, Cait," he whispered.

A hollow feeling settled in her chest. "I will try."

He pulled away slightly. A shadow crossed over his face. "Ewan is not the same man since he was wounded in battle. His family is worried, and so am I. I invited them to join us for Yule with the hope that coming together might lift his spirits. Ye know that we would never force ye, but please consider joining us at the high table when we welcome our guests." He pressed her hand to his heart. "For me, Cait."

She wanted to refuse him, to remain cloistered in her chamber where she could play her pipe and let the music wrap around her, blanketing her in beauty against the world she feared so much.

But the only thing greater than her fear was her love for her brothers.

"For ye, Matthew," she whispered.

A smile broke across his face as he scooped her into his muscular arms. "Thank ye, Cait!" He set her down quickly and cupped her cheeks. His eyes glinted with excitement. "Ye won't regret this. Ye'll see. This will be the most joyous Yuletide we've ever known."

Pasting a smile to her face, she gently pulled away from his touch. "I think I'll lie down for a while."

The exuberance in his posture and expression softened. A calm smile curved his lips. "I will leave ye then." He pressed a kiss to her cheek.

Her forced smile unwavering, she stood and watched his departure. When the door closed shut, she breathed out in a rush. Her heart pounded. Fear pulsed through her, inviting the sound of crashing waves, booming thunder, and endless screams to pummel her brain. Fighting the darkness that fought to consume her, she crossed to her bedside and picked up her pipe. Closing her eyes, she blew ribbons of melody that gently coiled around her, ethereal and as airy as a soft summer breeze. The beauty muffled the torment of her thoughts, until, at last, all she could hear was music.

Chapter Two

Laird Ewan MacLeod rocked side to side in his saddle, matching the rhythm of his horse's gait. He breathed deep the crisp winter air and smelled the snow he knew would soon fall, despite the warmth of the sunshine caressing his cold cheeks. Closing his useless eyes, he bent his head back, raising his face to the light he could not see.

"How far are we now from Castle Shéan?" he heard his mother ask.

Ewan's jaw clenched against the frustration Lady Alana's simple question stirred within him. He should have been able to provide her with an answer.

His shoulders tensed—he should be able to do a great many things, and less than a year ago was capable of just that. He had been laird to his people and a valiant warrior, his swordsmanship celebrated throughout the Highlands. But now, even the simplest task that the smallest child could perform was beyond him.

"Less than a league now, Mother," Ewan's brother answered quietly.

"Thank ye, Rowan," Lady Alana replied.

Silence hung thickly in the air. Ewan could only imagine the knowing glances his mother and brother were exchanging. He scowled, feeling his anger surge within him. At any moment, they would both try to start mending his tattered soul with the same tired platitudes they had been piling on him since he first lost his sight six months ago...

Ye're still the same man.

A laird is defined by his heart.

Everyone needs help, even the mightiest of warriors.

Ye're lucky to be alive.

Lady Alana cleared her throat.

"And so, it begins," Ewan muttered to himself.

"I cannot wait to see Matthew," she said to his surprise.

Ewan's shoulders eased, relieved to be spared from their so-called comfort, at least for the moment.

"Five years have passed since last he visited us at Castle Laoch," his mother continued. "Ye both know that I've always thought of him as my third son."

"Of course, ye do," Rowan replied. "He fostered with us from his eleventh birthday until he was a man grown."

"I wonder if he's chosen a bride yet..."

Ewan took a deep breath as he tried to block out their chatter. At that moment, second only to wanting his sight back, he wished he were home within the confines of his own keep. Somehow, he had been foolish enough to allow his brother to talk him into journeying to Castle Shéan.

A mirthless laugh fled his lips at his own thought.

It wasn't that Rowan's prattling on about the joys of spending Yuletide with the Campbells had managed to convince Ewan to concede, but rather, he relented so that he wouldn't have to keep listening to his brother's badgering. Now, he could not have regretted his decision more. Had he even a glimmer of hope of finding his own way back to MacLeod territory without another's aid, he would turn his horse around that very instant and leave his family to their merrymaking.

But there was precious little he could do now without someone's help.

Anger tightened his chest. He rested his hand on the hilt of his sword, soothed by the familiar touch of iron and leather. Trying to calm his rising ire, he forced his thoughts outward by listening to the world he could no longer see. Beneath the layer of his family's conversation, he discerned the rush of a river in the distance, and the rapid call of a Red Kite overhead. In his mind's eyes he could see the bird's reddish-brown color and angled wings. But then he stiffened as the pounding of hooves suddenly reached his ears.

"A rider comes this way," he snapped in his brother's direction.

"Worry naught," Rowan said, his voice placating, which only served to fuel Ewan's anger to new heights. "'Tis our own scout returning."

Ewan listened to the rhythmic sound as it grew louder.

"My laird!"

"What is it?" Ewan muttered in reply, recognizing the speaker as the captain of his guard. In his mind's eye, he saw Andrew with his plaited black hair and a thick scar puckering his cheek. The swordsman who left his mark on the captain would have taken Andrew's head had Ewan not been there to parry the enemy's next blow.

"The river crossing has flooded," Andrew said. "Which path shall we take now, my laird?"

"Why would ye put that question to me?" Ewan asked flatly.

"Thank ye, Captain," Rowan said quickly. "Keep right. Ye'll see a path that winds with the river. There is another crossing further down." After several moments of silence passed, Rowan cleared his throat. "Ewan, do ye approve this change of course?"

"Don't patronize me," Ewan shot in his brother's direction.

Silence filled the air. At length he heard Rowan say, "Ride ahead, Captain. Make certain the next crossing is clear."

The sound of retreating hoof beats reached Ewan's ears.

"Forgive me, brother," Rowan began, "but ye are laird. 'Tis only right that I seek yer approval."

Ewan jerked his horse to a halt. "Don't be ridiculous, Rowan. What am I to approve?" He pointed to his left. "Go that way, 'tis north." Then he pointed to his right. "Nay...nay...this way is north." He jerked his horse around. "Nay, this is the way!" His voice rose with his anger. "In case ye didn't realize, I cannot tell south from north, road from river. I'm liable to lead our men off a cliff as I am to find Castle Shéan."

"I meant no offense," Rowan answered stiffly. "I was only trying to be respectful."

"Then respect my wishes," Ewan snarled. "The sooner ye take the chiefdom from my useless hands, the happier I will be."

"We will not discuss this again," Lady Alana interjected. "Ye're my firstborn, Ewan. Ye're laird."

"I'm an invalid," Ewan said flatly. "I never should have come."

"Ye'll be glad ye did once we're there," Rowan said with forced brightness. "A change will do ye good."

"Nay, it won't. I'll be more dependent than ever. I will not be able to move about without falling on my face like a simpleton."

"Ye've been to Castle Shéan before."

"Aye, ten and three years ago."

"Ye will soon learn to navigate its rooms and corridors," Rowan assured him. "And we sent a missive to Laird Campbell with instructions for his servants not to move furnishings or leave stray items about."

Ewan snorted. "I'm certain Argyle is elated to be dictated as to what he can and cannot do in his own keep."

"Argyle is happy to welcome us into his home," Lady Alana insisted. "And ye will do well to remember that true friendship is unconditional."

"Thank ye, Mother," Ewan replied dryly. "I hope that ye also remembered to include my one condition in what I'm sure was a delightful missive."

"Aye," Rowan answered. "We gave specific instructions that there should be no trumpeters, no announcement, or any other ceremony upon our arrival."

Ewan nudged his horse forward. "At last one of my wishes has not been dismissed."

"In time, ye will feel differently about this visit," Rowan said quietly.

"And in time, ye will recognize the sentimental folly in yer own insistence that I remain laird."

Bitterness consumed him as he choked back the rage that set his heart to pound. He wanted to drive his heels into his horse's flanks and escape his family, escape the world. But he could not. He was imprisoned, held captive by his own worthless body. His hands closed into tight fists as he swallowed the growl of rage that barreled up his throat.

"Are ye all right, Ewan?" Lady Alana asked.

Nay, I'm alone in the darkness!

"Aye," he muttered. "I'm fine."

He expelled a long breath and hung his head, letting the music of the river fill his empty heart.

"CASTLE SHÉAN," LADY Alana exclaimed, causing Ewan to jerk upright.

"She's as beautiful as I remember," his mother continued.

Lady Alana's words cut Ewan's heart with sorrow. In his mind's eye, he could still see the home of his closest friend, which was known for its nine turreted towers. Four were positioned at each corner of the outer wall, and another four at the corners of the inner wall, surrounding the circular keep. But his favorite of the towers jutted out of the keep itself, making it the tallest point in Castle Shéan.

In his youth, he had accompanied Matthew when his foster brother had returned home to visit his family. Ewan had been just ten and five. He remembered himself in those days, strong, vital, his skill with a blade unmatched by any who trained with him. Laird Argyle Campbell had welcomed Ewan to Castle Shéan as if he were welcoming another son to his heart. He could still remember hunting parties, great feasts and games. But he could also remember the quieter occasions, which he had enjoyed no less. Evenings spent with the Campbell family in the solar, telling stories, and singing songs. A smile came unbidden to his lips as he suddenly remembered the youngest Campbell, Matthew's sister Cait. Ewan had never had a sister, and like her blood brothers, he, too, had doted on her.

In that moment, he was struck by the realization that she would be a woman grown. He quickly tallied the years since last he had set foot in Castle Shéan—ten and three. He blew out a slow breath, realizing that Cait would now be one and twenty.

"How quickly time passes," he said out loud.

"I told ye the journey here would take no time at all," Rowan chimed in not knowing the true meaning of Ewan's words.

Ewan did not reply, preferring to keep his thoughts trained on memories of a time when he had been whole and happy. A short while later, however, he was forced to abandon the past as the commotion of Castle Shéan reached his ears. Voices calling out words of welcome rained down from the battlements above, but at least he did not hear the flourish of trumpeters. Wood creaked, metal grated, and chains clanged as the drawbridge was lowered and the portcullis raised. More cheers and calls of greetings. Babies cried. Children laughed and squealed. Ewan's heart began to race as the din assaulted him from every direction. His chest tightened and a knot formed in the pit of his stomach.

"Welcome, Laird MacLeod," a deep voice boomed over the din, which Ewan recognized straightaway as belonging to the Chieftain of Clan Campbell. The image of a tall man with bushy black hair and a thick beard resting against his barreled chest flashed in Ewan's mind.

Ewan forced a smile to his lips. "Thank ye," he said, fighting the feeling of awkwardness as he did not know where to set his gaze and could only aim his eyes in the direction of Argyle's voice. "We needn't stand on formalities, Argyle."

"Indeed, we need not, Ewan."

Ewan jumped as a large hand suddenly patted his own. "'Tis only I," Argyle said quickly. "Let me help ye down."

Ewan stiffened. "I can manage," he said. Filled with dread, he slowly swung down from his horse. Instantly, he felt like a fool, standing amidst the bustle of the courtyard with no idea of what to do next or where to go.

"Ye've arrived just in time," Argyle said, forcing Ewan's thoughts to slow. "'Tis just five days now until Yule begins!"

Ewan forced a smile to his lips. "Indeed."

"Ewan!" a man cried the instant before Ewan's feet lifted clear off the ground, and he was pulled into a crushing embrace. He knew straightaway that it was Matthew's beefy arms and muscular frame that held him. The surrounding villagers cheered loudly—Ewan assumed at the affectionate display.

When Matthew set his feet down, Ewan swallowed hard against the panic building within him. He closed his eyes to quell the awkwardness of not being able to meet anyone's gaze.

"'Tis good to see ye," Matthew said.

A slight smile curved Ewan's lips. "I wish I could say the same."

"Ye're not missing much where I'm concerned. I'm hairier and thicker around the middle, but ye look well, Ewan. Ye're still as golden and beautiful as a maid."

"Well, that's something, isn't it," Ewan answered dryly. He cleared his throat, and shifted on his feet, listening for Rowan or his mother.

"I'm here," Rowan said in a quiet voice.

Relieved to feel his brother's hand on his arm, Ewan whispered. "Get me inside."

"Laird Argyle, Matthew, shall we make our way into Castle Shéan. Too long has it been since we've seen—" Rowan's words ended abruptly. "I mean—"

"It doesn't matter. Just get me inside," Ewan hissed. The din of the courtyard was too much.

"Lead on, Matthew," Rowan urged.

Keeping his head down, Ewan allowed his brother to lead him forward. Around him, people continued to call out greetings and blessings.

"We're coming up on the steps," Rowan said in a low voice. "First step...now."

Ewan swallowed hard and lifted his foot. He tried to keep his thoughts on the movement, one step, another step...

"Last step," Rowan whispered.

Ewan's heart hammered in his chest. "I never should have come."

"It will be all right," Rowan assured him.

"Nothing is all right," Ewan hissed. He fought back his anger, not wanting to embarrass himself further with an outburst in front of his friends.

Ewan followed Rowan's lead, feeling like a wave tumbling toward shore without control. Peter, Matthew's younger brother greeted Ewan warmly. Like all the Campbell children, Peter had black hair, but Ewan remembered that he was taller than both Matthew and Nathan, and leanly built. "Thank ye, Peter," Ewan murmured.

Person after person came forward, forcing Ewan to mumble niceties while he drowned in darkness and noise; that is, until he could bear it no longer. "I wish to be shone to my chamber," he blurted out loud to anyone who would listen.

"Straightaway, Laird MacLeod," Matthew said loudly.

"Ewan will do," he told his friend.

"Straightaway, Ewan," Matthew said, correcting himself. "This way."

Ewan felt reassured by the grip of Rowan's hand on his arm as they walked forward.

"More stairs," Rowan whispered. "First step...now."

Ewan could hear Matthew's footfalls in front of them.

"This is the final step," Rowan said. "I counted ten and seven in total."

Ewan nodded. They walked to the right. Their footsteps echoed in his mind. He longed to be at Castle Laoch where he knew the number of strides for every corridor and how to walk to any room he wished.

Finally, they stopped. He heard a door creak slightly as it opened. "'Tis our finest guest chamber," Matthew said.

"Thank ye." Ewan replied as he aimed his gaze in Matthew's direction. "We appreciate yer hospitality and the fineness of our welcome."

"Of course," Matthew said quickly. "No fanfare, no announcement or ceremony—just as ye requested."

"For which I am most grateful," Ewan said. "I do hope ye won't mind if I rest for a while. It was a long journey."

"Of course not," Matthew answered. "I shall come for ye when the dinner hour has arrived."

When Ewan heard the door shut, he stepped forward, but Rowan quickly seized his arm, gently pulling him in a different direction. "This way," his brother said.

Together, they took several strides. "Reach yer hand out," Rowan instructed him.

Ewan's fingers grazed soft wool.

"'Tis the bed," Rowan said.

"I realize that," Ewan answered.

"I counted six strides from the bed to the door."

"Not now." Ewan expelled a long breath as he slumped down on the bed and gripped his pounding head in his hands. But then a new sound pricked his ears. He straightened and canted his head, listening. "Do ye hear that?"

"What?" Rowan asked.

Like a dream, hazy and soft, Ewan discerned a faint melody. "'Tis music," he said. "Do ye not hear it?"

"I do, barely," Rowan answered. "Now, listen closely, Ewan. The hearth is over here. Right of the bed and four strides to reach a chair and a small side table."

His brother's words drowned out the pleasing sound. "I don't want to do this right now," he said.

Ignoring him, Rowan continued, "On the opposite side of the room, left of yer bed, is a wardrobe."

"Please go," Ewan said, clinging to his waning composure.

Rowan's footfalls sounded across the floor. "Five strides to reach the wardrobe, which opens from the—"

"Just go," Ewan snapped.

Moments passed in silence. Finally, Rowan said, "We'll continue later."

Ewan listened to his brother's retreating steps. When the door shut, he lay back on the bed and breathed out a slow breath as he fought for calm.

Again, the music came to him—a lone piper. The delicate sound was feather-soft and full of longing and heartache. Closing his eyes, he gave himself over to the raw beauty of the sound. Slowly, the chaos of their arrival and the feelings of utter helplessness began to fade from his thoughts until nothing remained but darkness—only now he wasn't alone. His companion was the uncanny music, the source of which he could not name. All he knew and, in that moment, all that mattered were the distant notes that touched his heart like a haunting refrain.

Chapter Three

Cait stood, clenching and unclenching her fists behind the screen, which separated the passage to the family rooms from the high dais. She licked her dry lips as she fought to calm her racing heart. The hum of simultaneous conversations punctuated by peals of laughter and calls of greetings reached her ears. She swallowed hard against the ache tightening her chest, the pressure increasing with every breathless moment she spent hiding, her feet frozen in place.

Why could she not conquer her fear?

Regret pummeled her already broken heart. She closed her eyes and struggled to remember another time, and what felt like another lass, when she had looked forward to feast days with youthful excitement.

As a child, she'd become anxious during the days leading up to any grand occasion—but not out of fear. In those days, impatience and anticipation would have been the causes for her restlessness while she counted down the final days until a great feast. And when the day at last would arrive, she'd awaken at the break of dawn, too excited to sleep.

But now...now, she was different.

She never took part in feast days, even when only members of Clan Campbell would be in attendance. In fact, she seldom left the family rooms within the keep, splitting her time between her chamber and the solar where she gathered with her brothers and father after the evening meal. As for her own meals, she typically ate those in the kitchen with Arlene, Castle

Shéan's plump, rosy-cheeked, and warmhearted cook, who had been like a mother to her since her own mother had passed away.

Willing her thoughts back to the present, she smoothed her hands down the front of her surcote. It was a soft blue, the color of the morning sky with intricate yellow needlework. She steeled her shoulders and forced her back to straighten. Determination was building within her, but then her breath hitched.

The chapel bell began to toll for the hour of *Vespers*, which meant that everyone was likely seated already.

Tears stung her eyes. If only she'd had the courage to come earlier, then people would have still been milling about, visiting and exchanging blessings of Yuletide. Her entrance might have even gone unnoticed. But now, surely everyone would bear witness to her arrival.

"There ye are!"

Sucking in a sharp breath, she turned and spied Helen hastening toward her. Cait swallowed hard, fighting to stop her tears.

"Oh, pet," Helen crooned while she lifted her apron and blotted at Cait's wet cheeks. "Now, ye listen to me," Helen began firmly. "Ye stand up straight and march out there with yer head held high."

Cait's chest tightened. "'Tis not as easy as that."

Helen cupped her cheeks and looked her hard in the eye. "I never said it would be easy. Still, ye must go, my lady."

Cait knew she was right.

Helen's expression softened. "The MacLeods are good folk. I've already had a lovely chat with Lady Alana. She is gentle."

"Is she? Are ye certain?"

"Aye, pet." Sadness laced Helen's voice, and her brows drew together before an encouraging smile brightened her face once more. "Ye can do this, my lady!"

Swallowing hard, Cait nodded. "I can do this," she repeated.

Helen nodded reassuringly.

Slowly, Cait straightened, forcing herself to stand tall. "For Matthew. I do this for Matthew."

"Nay, pet," Helen said, drawing her gaze. "Do it for yerself! Ye're so much more than ye allow yerself to be."

Tears once more flooded Cait's eyes. "I don't know how to be more."

"Blast," her maid cursed quietly. "Forget what I said. Go. Make yer entrance. Do it for Matthew."

Cait nodded. Holding her breath, she forced her feet to walk around to the other side of the screen. Straightaway, her gaze fixed on the high table whose occupants' backs were to her. When she saw the seating arrangements, she froze mid-step as the threads of courage to which she clung vanished.

Her brothers, Matthew and Peter, sat to her Father's left. The chair to the immediate right of her father, the rightful seat of the Lady of Castle Shéan, was empty. Meanwhile, occupying the seat next to the lady's chair, Cait's chair, was a man with long, golden hair and broad shoulders. She knew this seat of honor must be occupied by their guest, the Laird of Clan MacLeod. Seated next to him on his right was a woman, slim of figure and wearing layers of sheer veils, who she knew must be Ewan's mother, Lady Alana. To her right, clad in the MacLeod plaid, sat another man with dark blond hair. Her gaze darted across the length of the high table once more.

There was only one empty seat. The lady's chair betwixt her father and Laird MacLeod.

She had assumed she'd be safely wedged between Matthew and Peter. If she had known that she would be seated next to one of the guests, she never would have agreed to join the festivities—even for Matthew.

Her gaze returned to the back of the man sitting in the chair next to hers. Suddenly, a fleeting memory stole into her thoughts of a handsome lad with golden hair. He was laughing as he chased her playfully around the table in the solar. The memory made her heart lighten ever so slightly. She closed her eyes, and another memory of the same lad flashed in her mind's eye—he was squatting down and opening his arms to her.

Hush now, Cait. Don't cry. I'm here.

Once upon a time, she had been very fond of Ewan MacLeod, and she could still remember how he had been the only one able to soothe her during a fierce storm. She swallowed hard, wishing he could now quell the tempest raging in her mind. Taking a deep breath, she fought to hold on to the comforting memory, but the distant joy was no match for her fear. Her heart pounding, she took a step back.

"'Tis Lady Cait!"

Her breath hitched.

Anna, one of the young maids serving the high table had seen her. Anna's unbound red curls bounced as she waved at Cait.

Everyone turned in their chairs to look at her, all except for Ewan. Smiles broke across their faces. Her father stood and hastened toward her. His face beamed with pride. "Ye look beautiful." He cupped her cheek and in a soft voice said, "Yer presence here fills my heart." As if to prove his claim, tears flooded her father's eyes. "Come," Argyle said, offering her his arm.

As they approached the high table, the rest of the great hall came into view. Garlands of holly hung over rows of trestle tables, teaming with her kinfolk, which stretched from just beyond the entryway nigh to the high dais. As she drew close, the hum of conversation ceased. Her gaze scanned the faces, some familiar and others less so, but each one wore the same shocked expression—eyes wide, mouths agape. Silence settled over the room but only for a moment. An instant later, her kin stood and cheered. She stiffened. Her face burned.

"Ye needn't be frightened, lass," her father whispered. "Yer people love ye. It isn't every day that they are given a glimpse of their lady."

Her face continued to burn, and her legs felt as if her bones had gone soft. When they reached the high table, her brothers and the man in the seat farthest to the right pushed their chairs back and stood, while both Ewan and his mother remained seated.

"Smile, Cait," Matthew said in a low voice.

Cait forced a smile to her lips and gave an awkward wave at her people before shifting her gaze to the floor. Her father pulled her chair out. She quickly sat down.

"Forgive me for not standing," Laird MacLeod said, leaning close.

Her heart raced. "Ye...ye needn't apologize," she replied, hating the tremble in her voice.

She cast a sidelong glance at him. Because of his reputation as a fierce warrior, she had expected him to have grown into a man built more like her father and Matthew, wide with thick, bulky muscles, but to her relief, he was made more like her brothers Peter and Nathan—tall and strong but sleek.

"Daughter."

She shifted her gaze to look up at her father who had yet to reclaim his seat. "Allow me to introduce, Laird Ewan MacLeod."

Swallowing hard, she shifted her gaze back to their guest. A smile slightly curved Ewan's lips, but his eyes remained closed.

He dipped his head in her direction. "Just Ewan if ye please, and we've already met."

She could feel her cheeks warm again. "Aye, we have," she said, although her reply was barely more than a whisper.

"I'm glad ye remember him," her father said brightly. Then, he gestured to the lady beside Ewan. "Lady Alana, my daughter, Cait."

Leaning to see past her son, Lady Alana smiled. "Good eventide, my lady."

Cait dipped her head respectfully. "Welcome to Castle Shéan, my lady," she said, and was pleased that her words came out with greater strength.

"And lastly, Rowan, Lady Alana's second son, has joined us for the Yule season as well."

She met Rowan's warm gaze. His eyes were green, and his hair was a darker shade of blond than Ewan's. He smiled. "'Tis a pleasure to finally meet ye, my lady. Matthew has spoken of ye with great fondness all the long years that we've known him."

She dipped her head. "Welcome," she managed to say.

Then her father retook his seat and slid the trencher in front of him over so that they could share. "Ye must be famished, Cait."

On the contrary, her stomach felt as if it were twisted in knots, but at least eating gave her something with which to be occupied. Her hand shook as she reached for a crust of bread. Embarrassed, she glanced at Ewan to see if he had noticed, but his eyes remained shut. In that moment, she remembered what Matthew had told her.

Six months ago, Ewan was injured in battle. The wound had festered, and he burned with fever. In the end, God spared his life but took his sight. She looked at him sidelong. There was a gentleness to his features. He had a straight nose and a generous mouth. His lips were full and sensual. His flaxen hair fell thickly down his back, and his skin was bronzed by the sun. He had yet to open his eyes. Despite how she searched her memory, she could not remember their color. Both Lady Alana and Rowan had green eyes, but she felt quite certain his were different.

She nibbled on a piece of bread as she continued to study his features while he and her father discussed last season's harvest. When he spoke, his voice was pleasing to her ears, deep and masculine but gentle. Her nerves eased slightly, although not enough that she dared to scan the trestle tables in front of her. She could feel the villagers' gazes fixed on her. Still, the longer she listened to the affable tone of Ewan's voice, the more at ease she became. Before long, the tension began to release from her shoulders. Then, to her surprise, Ewan leaned close and hummed softly in her ear. In that moment, she realized that she had been humming to herself.

Blushing, she stopped.

"Ye have a lovely voice," Ewan said softly.

She dipped her head to acknowledge his kind words, but then realized he would not be able to see the motion. "Thank ye," she whispered.

"Do ye like music?"

She swallowed, wishing his attention was still trained on her father. "I do," she answered simply.

"What else do ye enjoy?"

Her chest tightened slightly. She did not wish to talk about herself. Silence stretched between them until, at last, she blurted, "Tell me of Castle Laoch?

A slight smile curved his lips. "I also do not enjoy speaking of myself," he said knowingly. "But Castle Laoch..." His voice took on a wistful note. "Well, that's a different matter altogether."

He began to tell her about the beauty of his keep and the surrounding lands. She closed her eyes while she listened to him speak of sinuous rivers and rolling moors with the pride of a laird who loved his land and his people.

"Blast," he cursed loudly.

Alarmed, her eyes flew open.

His chalice had overturned. Wine spilled onto both their laps.

Rowan and Lady Alana were on their feet an instant later as were her father and brothers; meanwhile, Anna rushed toward them with rags in hand.

"Damn it!" Ewan snapped, his voice harsh. He shoved his chair back to stand but Anna was right behind him. She cried out as she fell back on the high dais.

"What's going on?" Ewan shouted. His bronzed skin was suddenly red and mottled.

Cait's heart pounded.

An abrasive choir rent the air as the villagers pushed back their benches to have a better view of the high table. Cait's gaze darted around the room, passing over prying gazes and wide eyes.

Rowan grabbed Ewan's arm. "'Tis all right."

"Nothing is all right," Ewan snarled as he snaked his arm away.

Matthew and Argyle tried to calm their guest down. Everyone was speaking at once. Cait's breath fled her body. The chaos and raised voices made her heart race harder. Soon, the screams in her own mind joined the din. Tears stung her eyes. She could take it no longer. Covering her face with her hands she raced toward the family rooms. But as the noise of the great hall began to fade, the storm in her own mind grew louder—thunder roared, waves crashed, and the screams...

"My lady what has happened?" Helen cried as Cait raced past her.

She did not stop to answer. Breathless, she hastened down the hall past several chamber doors until she reached her own stairwell. Hitching her tunic high, she wound her way up the narrow steps to her tower chamber and shut the door. Her chest heaving, she pressed her back against the slatted wood of the closed door. The sound of Ewan's harsh voice echoed in her mind, louder than the thunder and howling wind that endlessly plagued her memory. Tears stung her eyes. In his youth, Ewan may have been patient and amiable, but it was clear to her now that he had grown into an angry man with a fierce temper.

On wobbly legs, she crossed to her bedside table and took up her pipe. The first notes were sobs, raw and sharp as she fought to catch her breath. Then, slowly, the sound changed. She let her fingers move along the pipe of their own accord; until at last, a melody rose out of the chaos. The song wrapped around her, blanketing her soul. Soon, her heart ceased to race and her mind emptied and all that remained was music.

EWAN SAT SLUMPED OVER on the edge of an unfamiliar bed in a chamber of a castle leagues from his own.

"Can I bring ye anything?" Rowan asked.

Ewan shook his bowed head.

"Listen, Ewan, do not fash yerself about tonight. No one blames ye for—"

"Just go, Rowan."

When he heard his brother retreat and the chamber door close, Ewan gripped his head in his hands. He was awash in humiliation. Self-loathing filled him, burning through his heart to his very soul. So tight was his chest that his breaths came in shallow gasps as he stood. His restless pain ached for release, but he could not ride it off, racing over the moors on his mighty steed, nor could he go to the training fields and spar with his men.

He turned in a circle, his eyes searching, but there was nothing. No light. No path for escape. Only darkness. A snarl of fury tore from his lips. How he longed to break free from his own skin.

Pain gripped his heart as he felt for the bed. Slumping on the edge again, he hung his head, willing his mind to disappear into a void, but his thoughts refused to empty. Instead an image came to him of a woman with long black hair. He could not discern her features in the haze nor her true outline. She was like a ghost...

A mirthless laugh escaped his lips as he realized his mind had conjured the only image of a grownup Cait that he would ever know—a vague assumption as if he were seeing her from behind a veil, like one of the fae.

He tried to shake the image from his thoughts, but something more tangible came to his mind.

Her voice.

Soft. Timid. Nothing like the outspoken lass he had known in his youth.

He couldn't help but wonder what ill fate had befallen her to make her so nervous and withdrawn. Years ago, he recalled hearing rumors of a scandal, but he had never given an ear to gossip, especially when the subjects were dear to him.

Still, he had been surprised to hear the tremble in her voice when she had joined the high table. Instantly, her timidity had struck a chord in his heart, bringing his protective nature to the fore.

Now, sitting on the edge of his bed, he closed his eyes and allowed himself to savor those brief moments. Over the course of their exchange her voice had become gradually stronger. He had even made her laugh, the sound hesitant but beautiful, stirring his desire. So great was his sudden attraction that he had forgotten he was no longer whole; that is, until he clumsily knocked over his chalice. He closed his hands into tight fists as once again rage, heavy and violent, raked his very bones, silencing the feminine laughter in his mind.

What a fool he was.

His thoughts had no business lingering on Cait, no matter how light she had briefly made him feel. How could he care for a wife when he could no longer care for himself?

Darkness replaced the hazy feminine image in his mind as he lay back on the bed and expelled a long breath. He would talk to Rowan on the morrow. After this eventide, he did not doubt that Rowan would see the folly of bringing him to Castle Shéan.

Numbness slowly moved through him, quieting the sorrow.

But then a faint melody crept into his mind, soft and silken.

He sat up and trained his ear to the sound, letting it gently coil around him. The notes were insistent and calming, making him feel as though he was no longer alone. Standing, he counted the strides to his chamber door. Easing it open, he listened but heard no footfalls nearby.

"Hello," he said in a soft voice.

Only silence answered.

Keeping his hand on the rough stone wall of the corridor, he walked toward the sound, counting the strides as he went to ensure he could find his way back to his chamber. Slowly, he progressed, the faint sound growing louder as he went. The wall beneath his hand suddenly disappeared. He outstretched his hand further, expecting to find a door, but there was nothing. Bending low, he reached down. This time he traced the shape of a stairwell, but he dared not climb and lose track of his own chamber. The last thing he wanted was the humiliation of wandering into another's room. He slid down and sat on one of the first steps.

The music was clear now. The notes flowed through him, gently soothing the places within him that ached most.

He lay his head against the wall and released a long breath. "Thank ye," he whispered out loud to the piper...*for sitting with me the darkness.*

Chapter Four

Cait's stomach rumbled. She set her needlework down on the table beside her chair and stood. Stretching her arms over her head, she took a deep breath. She hadn't left her room for two full days. The solitude had brought her peace from the discord and chaos that had sent her fleeing from the great hall, but now, she was beginning to feel restless. Humming to keep her thoughts away from dark places, she began to tidy her things, placing several spools of thread neatly in her sewing basket. Then she straightened her bedding, which she had rumpled when taking an afternoon nap.

Once again, her stomach voiced its need. Helen would be along soon enough with a supper tray for her, but Cait was admittedly looking for a little company. Knowing that their guests would join her family in the solar following the feast, she could not count on seeing her brothers. Instead, she decided to take her evening meal with Arlene. Cait descended the winding stairwell and peered into the hallway to ensure it was empty before hastening to the servants' stairwell that led to the kitchen.

As she neared the bottom of the stairs, she spotted Arlene's plump figure and silver streaked chestnut hair among the many undercooks and serving lassies who were darting around the kitchen, their arms laden with steaming trenchers and tankards brimming with ale. The delicious smell of fresh baked bannock made her stomach growl again. Keeping hidden in the stairwell, she waited for Arlene to look up and notice her. In the midst of so much bustling activity, she settled down to wait on one of the steps, knowing it could be some time before Castle Shéan's cook would be able to rest and have her own supper.

Finally catching the cook's eye, Cait waved and hastened down the stairs. "Will ye dine with me, Arlene?"

Arlene dabbed at the sweat on her brow. "Under normal circumstances, ye ken I would, my lady, but there are only a few days left before the first feast of Yule, and I wish to eat in the great hall with our kin." A smile lit Arlene's warm, green eyes. "Why don't ye join us again?"

Cait forced a smile to her lips. "I would rather not, but ye go ahead and enjoy yerself."

She started to turn away, but then she noticed Anna, whose face was nearly as red as her hair, scowling on the other side of the room at Eleanor, whose thick black brows were equally as furrowed. Curious about their disagreement, Cait crossed to stand beside Arlene.

Arlene followed her gaze. "Och, just ignore them, pet. I am. They're fighting over who will bring Laird MacLeod his tray. I've told them that they must work it out themselves, or else they will both have to go."

Cait drew closer to the maids, pretending to be occupied with stirring the pottage while she listened to their argument.

"I took his dinner tray," Anna hissed.

Eleanor tossed her long, black plait over her shoulder before setting her hands on her hips. "Aye, 'tis true, but if I do recall, ye told me that he merely grunted when ye entered the room. But when I brought his breakfast tray, he yelled at me for not announcing myself sooner."

"Well, I don't care to be yelled at," Anna said, crossing her arms over her chest.

"Aye, well I don't care to be yelled at again!"

Cait returned to where Arlene was adding roughly cut herbs to a large pot of boiling water. "I do not blame them for being scared of Laird MacLeod. His outburst the other night terrified me."

Arlene met her gaze. Cait could tell that the cook had something on her mind, but the older woman merely shrugged and turned back to her task.

Cait's gaze darted around the room for a moment. Had she done something wrong? It was not she who had lost her temper. "Have I upset ye?"

Arlene's face softened. "Nay, pet, of course not. I was in the great hall when the incident happened. I saw how upset ye were by the chaos and raised voices." Arlene lifted her shoulders. "'Tis just that...well..." her words trailed off.

Cait gently took Arlene's hand. "Ye know I value yer guidance above all others. If I've done something wrong, please...I wish to know."

Arlene cupped her cheek lovingly. "Ye've done nothing wrong, but neither did Laird MacLeod. Ye of all people should be able to show him the compassion he deserves. Like ye, he is no stranger to suffering. Can ye imagine how it must feel to be a warrior and laird, and then suddenly to be so helpless?"

A pang of compassion cut straight through Cait's heart. She closed her eyes and felt the weight of the bleak darkness. She knew what it was to be trapped in the dark. In that moment, she realized how terrified and alone Ewan must feel. Then, her mind returned to the lovely moments they had shared at the high table. How calm his simple conversation had made her. Her own fear had been eased by his gentle attention.

In that moment, she knew that Arlene was right. Anger had not guided his behavior after he knocked his chalice over. Fear, confusion, shame...he must have felt all the same emotions that plagued her every day of her life.

Suddenly, her heart ached for him.

She looked over to where Anna and Eleanor stood arguing. Then, taking a deep breath, she said, "I will take Laird MacLeod his tray."

Both lassies turned and looked at her with wide eyes. "Nay, my lady. Ye mustn't," Anna blurted.

"Please don't go, my lady," Eleanor pleaded. "I will do it. I will go!"

"Lassies," Arlene interrupted sternly, setting her hands on her hips. "Yer lady has spoken. Will ye not heed her wishes?"

An instant later, both Anna and Eleanor hung their heads.

"Forgive us, my lady," Eleanor said humbly, dipping in a low curtsy.

"That's better," Arlene said. "Now, both of ye run along and see if anyone's tankard needs filling."

When the lassies had seized the pitchers of ale and left the room, Cait turned to Arlene. "Ye needn't admonish them on my account. I'm not truly lady of Castle Shéan."

Arlene's eyes flashed wide. "Are ye not?"

Cait shook her head.

"My lady, I remember the day ye were born. I can remember the first moment I saw ye cradled in yer mother's arms—the arms of the lady of Castle Shéan."

"But that's just it—I'm nothing like my mother. I'm too..." Cait's words trailed off.

"Too what?" the cook demanded.

"Broken," Cait said quietly.

Arlene pointed to the pot boiling over the fire. "Ye ken what I'm going to say to ye."

Cait sighed. "I ken. 'Tis yer favorite pot."

"Aye, my favorite pot, but some of the undercooks have complained that it is dented. And what have I told them?"

Cait took a deep breath. "Ye can still boil water in a dented pot."

Arlene cupped Cait's cheek. "Ye are the Lady of Castle Shéan." The plump woman turned and picked up the tray of food off the table and handed it to Cait. "And I am proud of ye. Now, run along before Laird MacLeod's supper gets cold."

Nodding, Cait turned and made her way toward the servant's stairwell and back the way she'd come. When she reached his chamber door, she took a deep breath. It was then she noticed that it was slightly ajar. Peering inside, she saw him sitting in a chair at an open casement. His head was resting on the back of the chair and his eyes were closed. His features were so serene, she wondered whether he slept.

Quietly, she eased the door open and softly padded into the room, making her way to the table next to where he sat.

"Good evening, Lady Cait."

She froze. Her heart started to race. "How did ye know it was me?"

He remained still but for the smile that played at his lips. "Ye smell of lavender and honey."

Her hands started to shake, rattling the items on the tray.

He jerked upright. "I did not mean to frighten ye."

Setting the tray down, she clenched her fists to keep them steady. "Ye didn't frighten me. I...I'm just nervous."

He kept his eyes closed. "Then I'm sorry to make ye nervous."

She clenched and unclenched her fists. "It isn't yer fault. I'm nervous most of the time."

His gaze still downcast, he motioned in front of him. "If I remember correctly, there is a chair about two strides to yer right. Would ye like to join me?"

Her heart raced faster than ever. She cast her gaze toward the open door and then to the chair. She swallowed hard but held fast to her courage. "I will sit for a spell."

He smiled. Warmth flooded his cheeks. And for the first time, he opened his eyes.

Her breath caught. They were golden brown as bright as amber. In that moment, seeing his beautiful smile and striking gaze, her memories of him flooded back to her.

He canted his head to the side. "Lady Cait, I'm quite certain that ye're still standing."

A nervous laugh fled her lips. "Ye're correct." Taking a deep breath, she crossed to the chair and sat. An instant later, he reached back, feeling for the arm of the chair, and then he, too, sat but on the edge of his seat.

"I'm happy that ye're here," he said, his expression serious. "I've been wanting to speak with ye about what happened the other evening. I know that I frightened ye when I lost my temper. I shouldn't have done so, and I'm sorry—"

"Please don't apologize," she blurted. Then in a quieter voice, she said, "Ye didn't do anything wrong."

He shook his head. "My reaction was inexcusable. The same can be said for my foul mood these last two days."

"Nay," she insisted. "Ye were overwhelmed and rightly so."

A shadow crossed his face as he eased back in his seat. "Imagine, a laird overwhelmed by an overturned chalice."

"Forgive me, Laird MacLeod, but 'tis not as simple as that." Her chest tightened. "I ken what ye felt...or at least I think I do."

He straightened in his seat. "What did I feel?"

She took a deep breath to fuel her courage. "Trapped," she said, her voice barely above a whisper.

Then he shifted his body and leaned toward her. "Ye're right," he answered quietly. Perched on the edge of his seat, he closed his eyes. "In those dark moments, I'm, as ye said, trapped, and my instinct is to fight my way free." A scowl darkened his beautiful countenance for a moment, but an instant later, the emotion fled his face. His expression became impassive. He held up his hands in resignation. "No sword can slay this foe...for it is I...I am my own enemy."

She shook her head, and then remembered that he could not see the gesture. "That isn't true," she said softly.

He blew out a rush of air and sat back once more. "Ye're right again. I'm not the enemy, nor am I the hero...not anymore. I ken what I am. The truth is that I'm broken."

She sat straight. "Nay, ye're not broken." Suddenly, Arlene's words came to her. "Ye're just...dented, and ye ken what they say about a dented pot?"

He lifted his face, and once more, she was struck by the beauty of his unseeing eyes. "Nay, I'm not familiar with that one."

Her heart quickened. She swallowed hard, afraid to say the words she had so often heard but never truly understood until that moment. "Ye can still boil water in a dented pot," she said in a rush.

He sat very still for a moment before he started to shake slightly. For a moment, she thought she had brought him to tears. But then, he chuckled, and an instant later, he threw his head back and started to laugh. The sound was deep and rich.

A smile broke across her face. Then laughter bubbled up her own throat. She covered her mouth with her hands, but the noise burst past her fingers. Her laughter rang out, mingling with his in a joyous chorus. Soon, tears were streaming down her cheeks, but they held no sadness. Sitting back, she rested her arms across her stomach and caught her breath.

"I can't remember the last time I laughed so hard," he said, a smile brightening his face.

"Nor can I," she said breathlessly.

For several moments, neither spoke, but the silence wasn't heavy. It was as light and comfortable as a summer breeze.

"Ewan, may I ask ye something?"

"Of course."

She gripped the arms of her chair to fuel her courage. "Ewan, do ye remember that time when I was just a wee lass and a storm rolled in off the moors?"

He chuckled. "Aye, I do. Ye were frightened by the thunder. So, I gathered ye up in my arms and we sat near the hearth in the solar." Again, he laughed. "Ye asked me to sing ye a song, and then another and another. Eventually, I ran out of tunes I knew, and I had to start making them up."

She laughed. "I remember. Ye made every song about a wee lass named Cait."

His rich laughter again filled the room. "That's right." Then he sang, his voice deep and pleasing, "There once was a wee lass named Cait who would never wish me for a mate. Because she's marrying her brother who is as hairy as her father, and so, that is her fate."

Cait was laughing so hard that, once more, tears streamed down her cheeks. "I had forgotten how I always said I would marry Matthew." She chuckled. "He is still my favorite, although don't tell Peter or Nathan I said so."

He smiled. "Yer secret is safe." Once again, he shifted to the edge of his seat as a tentative expression came over his face. "Cait, can I ask a favor of ye?"

"Of course," she answered.

"In my mind ye're still that wee lass. I would never ask a new acquaintance this, but since ye and I are old friends...would ye allow me to touch yer face?"

The idea of being touched by Ewan made her breath catch. "All right." She swallowed hard. "Shall I come closer?"

"Nay," he said. "I will come to ye."

He stood. Her gaze raked over his tall, powerful build. Her heart quickened as he stepped forward, stopping in front of her. She gripped the arms of her chair as he knelt in front of her, his face suddenly level with her own.

"Do ye need me to guide ye," she asked her voice barely above a whisper.

A slight smile curved his lips. "Yer voice already has."

Then he slowly reached out. Her breath caught as his fingertips gently grazed her cheek. His touch feather-soft, he glided his fingers along her jaw line. Then he slowly traced the shape of her mouth and nose. She closed her eyes and drew a tremulous breath while he outlined her brows.

"Ye're beautiful," he whispered, his breath hot against her cheek.

"Nay," she breathed as her face suddenly burned. Her heart hammered in her chest.

He cupped her face gently in his large, calloused hands. "But ye are, Cait, just as I always knew ye'd be, inside and out."

"There is nothing beautiful inside me," she murmured, hardly aware of what she was saying.

He stiffened. "But ye're wrong. Ye have so much beauty within ye."

And in that moment, she could not argue, for his touch had, indeed, awakened something deep inside her—something beautiful, smoldering, and exciting. Her soul drank in the comfort of his nearness. She felt completely safe and utterly vulnerable all at the same time.

One of his hands coursed down, stroking her neck. "Yer pulse is racing."

"Is it?" she said, licking her dry lips.

"Why do ye think that is?" he asked, his voice low and husky.

She stood abruptly. Her legs trembled. "I should go," she blurted.

"Wait," he rasped. His hand clasped her arm, then softly trailed down to take her hand in his. He stood and a slow sideways smile lifted one side of his mouth. Then he dipped his head to her. "Allow me to thank ye before ye take yer leave. I can't remember the last time I passed such a pleasant evening."

A smile came unbidden to her lips. "Nor can I," she managed to reply before stepping from his grasp.

"Sweet dreams, Ewan," she said softly.

"Sweet dreams, fair Cait."

As she crossed the room on unsteady legs, a fresh sadness entered her heart, but it was not caused by painful memories. Instead, she felt as if her heart was being pulled by a tangible bond that existed between them, a bond that she had forgotten until that night. It almost hurt to leave his company. At the door, she stopped and took one last glance back. Her gaze trailed over his face. She savored the inherent strength of his rugged features. Drawing a deep breath, she stepped into the corridor, all the while longing set her heart afire. When she returned to her room, she took up her pipe. The music that flowed through her caressed the night with silken notes and sensual rhythms and made her dream of old friends and new-found beauty.

Chapter Five

E wan awoke to a soft rapping on the door. Slowly, he sat up and stretched his neck from side to side. Having slept very little the night before, his head felt heavy. But then he straightened, becoming suddenly alert. There was a chance, however slight, that the person seeking to gain entrance to his chamber was Cait.

Quickly adjusting the blanket to ensure he was covered up to his waist, he called out, "Enter."

Training his ear toward the door, he listened for her soft footfalls.

"I've come to replenish yer hearth, Laird MacLeod." The voice belonged to a young lad.

The excited tension eased from Ewan's shoulders as he listened to the hurried steps.

"Thank ye and good morrow," Ewan replied.

"Good morrow, Laird MacLeod."

Ewan swung his legs over the side of the bed and took a deep, easy breath and smiled, feeling a lightness in his chest for the first time in a long while. A quiet sigh escaped his lips as he leaned his head back and let the memory of Cait's laughter wash over him. Her departure from his chamber the night before had been sudden, and clearly, she had been tentative and nervous throughout their exchange. Still, the intimacy that had passed between them as he had traced the soft contours of her beautiful face was undeniable. She had responded to his touch; this he did not doubt.

Once again, anticipation pulsed through him as he stood and turned in the direction of the hearth. "My good lad, what is yer name?"

"Timothy," the boy answered.

Judging by his voice, Ewan guessed the lad to be older than ten years but not as many as four and ten. "What is the hour, Timothy?"

"'Tis *Prime*, Laird MacLeod," the lad replied.

"Ewan will suffice, thank ye," he said absently as he stood and crossed to the wardrobe, counting the steps as he went. At any moment, his brother would arrive and offer to lead him to the great hall to break their fast and, unlike the past two days, not only did he intend to accept Rowan's aid—he wished to be ready so that they could head straight to the high dais. The prospect of seeing Cait again brought a smile to his face that he could not contain as he felt for his shirt and pulled the finely woven linen over his head. The he took up his plaid and belt. Fumbling with the buckle, it took him several attempts to secure the bottom folds of his plaid to his waist, but for the first time since losing his sight, he breathed through the frustration and refused the usual disparaging thoughts that always plagued him when completing simple tasks.

When the top folds of his plaid were secured over his shoulder, he turned around and crossed to his bed, sat down on the edge, and slowly laced his knee-length brogues. Turning his head in the direction of the hearth, he said, "Timothy."

"Aye, Laird MacLeod."

"Has Lady Cait made her way to the high table this morrow?"

"Nay, Laird MacLeod."

"Ewan will suffice," Ewan said again.

"Forgive me, Laird Mac—er...Ewan."

Ewan smiled. "Well done, Timothy. Now, tell me this. At which hour does yer lady typically break her fast?"

"A tray is brought to her chamber at *Prime*."

Ewan's smile faltered. "She does not eat with the family?"

"Nay, Laird...er...Ewan."

Ewan scrubbed a hand over his face. "Then I must wait until the dinner hour to see her," he muttered out loud.

"Forgive me, Ewan," Timothy began, "But Lady Cait does not take any of her meals in the great hall."

Ewan's brows drew together. "Does she not?"

"Never. She mostly keeps to her chamber and the solar, and the kitchen, of course, as she's especially fond of Arlene."

"Who is Arlene?"

"Castle Shéan's cook."

Ewan shook his head. The lad wasn't making any sense. "Ye must be mistaken, for she attended the supper three evenings past."

"Aye," the lad said in a rush. "I couldn't believe my eyes when I saw her walk out onto the high dais. No one could. And the next day, I heard some of the serving lassies talking in the kitchen. They said she came down for supper as a special favor to Matthew."

Ewan's chest tightened. "Blast," he cursed, his heart suddenly heavy with remorse.

"My laird, did I do something wrong?" the lad asked.

Ewan took a deep breath. "Nay, Timothy. 'Tis I who am at fault. My outburst during the meal must have terrified yer lady."

He stood straight, determination imbuing his stance. "But no matter, dented pot and all that. I will make amends."

"If ye've a dented pot, I can try to hammer it out," Timothy said eagerly. "I'm going to start apprenticing soon under the smithy."

Ewan smiled, hearing the pride in the young lad's voice. "I'm certain ye will make an excellent blacksmith one day, and I thank ye for the offer, Timothy. But this is one dent a hammer can't fix."

"'Tis good to see ye up and about!" called a booming voice from the direction of the doorway.

Ewan shifted his stance. "Good morrow, Matthew!"

"A good morrow, indeed!" Matthew's heavy footfalls sounded, guiding Ewan to his friend. Matthew clamped his hand on Ewan's shoulder. "'Tis glad I am to see ye looking so well."

Ewan smiled. "I'll just have to take yer word for it." His mind was racing with questions about Cait. Ewan paused to gather his bearings before gesturing in the direction of the hearth. "Have a seat, Matthew. There is much to discuss."

"Indeed, there is," Matthew replied. "But I was hoping to do so from a different sort of seat."

"Ye wish to go for a ride," Ewan said knowingly.

"Aye," Matthew answered. "'Tis a fine morning. Cold but clear."

Ewan listened to Matthew's footfalls crossing the room and heard the wardrobe door open, then shut a moment later.

"Here's yer cloak."

"Thank ye." Ewan swept the heavy wool over his shoulders and said, "I'm ready, but I'll need yer arm."

Matthew led him from his chamber, through the keep, and out into the courtyard where Ewan breathed deep the crisp, wintry air.

"'Tis a fine, clear day," Rowan said, suddenly appearing at his side.

Ewan dipped his head in the direction of his brother's voice. "Indeed, it is."

"Yer mount is saddled and ready." Rowan brought Ewan's stallion close and handed him the reins, which he followed until his fingers found the bridle. Then he pressed his cheek to his horse's muzzle.

"Ye look well today," Rowan said.

A slight smile curved Ewan's lips. "I would say the same to ye if I could."

Rowan chuckled. "Did ye sleep well?"

"I hardly slept at all," Ewan answered honestly. He had been up most of the night listening to the piper and thinking about Cait. In that moment, an image surfaced in his thoughts. Touching the contours of her face had allowed the hazy fog to clear, and he saw her in his mind's eye. Black hair shining, full lips parted, a pert nose and high cheek bones set in an oval canvas, delicate and soft.

"I'm ready," he said, eager to be on their way so that he and Matthew could discuss Cait in private. After he pulled himself into the saddle, they bade Rowan farewell and set out at a trot. A cold breeze cut through his cloak, but after two days of remaining isolated in his chamber, he felt awakened by the chill.

"It snowed a wee bit," Matthew said, his words suddenly measured, and his voice stilted.

A feeling of foreboding washed over Ewan, and he knew then why Matthew had wished to take him for a ride. "I ken what's on yer mind, Matthew. So why don't ye just say yer piece and get it over with."

Moments passed. Ewan listened to the crunching of the horses' hooves on the frozen bracken to keep him from snapping at his friend, who clearly was searching for the right words with which to meddle.

Finally, Matthew spoke, "This business about ye giving up the chiefdom has to stop."

Ewan shook his head, expelling a long breath. Just as he had thought. No doubt Rowan and his mother had solicited Matthew's aid in trying to convince Ewan to remain laird, despite his inability to carry out his duties. "Did ye forget that only a short while ago, ye had to fetch my cloak for me from my wardrobe, or that I had to hold yer arm simply to walk to the courtyard."

"That matters not."

"That is everything," Ewan shot back, feeling his anger flare. "How can I lead my men into battle if I can't even see the enemy?"

"That is why ye have a captain."

"Is that what yer father does?" Ewan scoffed. "He sits on his throne in his keep while his men march to battle?"

"That's different."

"Exactly," Ewan hissed. "I'm different. I'm not the same man."

"Give yerself more time. Yer soul will heal, and ye will come to know how strong ye still are."

"My sight isn't coming back. The passing of time means naught," Ewan said flatly.

"I ken yer sight will not return, but time will heal the rest of ye. And ye'll be a better man for yer struggles."

Ewan shook his head. "I've had this conversation enough times with Rowan and my mother. My strength and reputation with a sword were once an asset to my people. Now, my weakness will only encourage ill fortune. How will I protect our lands and our coffers? How will I safeguard their lives?"

"Ewan—"

"That's enough, Matthew. Ye've said yer piece, and I've said mine. I am only thinking of what is best for my people."

"Are ye? Or is fear guiding yer actions?"

Ewan jerked on the reins of his horse, bringing his mount to a halt. "Only a fool wouldn't be afraid. I'm no fool, and neither are ye. So, do not speak to me as if ye could know what it is to be in my position."

He waited for Matthew to reply, but his friend did not speak at first. At length, Matthew said, "Ye're right. I cannot know yer struggle firsthand. But I am also right—yer people need ye. Ye're their laird."

Ewan lifted his shoulders. "Then we are at an impasse and must accept that on this point we disagree."

"Fine," Matthew muttered. "I will abandon the matter...for now."

"Good," Ewan said brightly. "Because there is another subject that I wish to discuss with ye."

Matthew did not reply straightaway, betraying his reluctancy to change the subject. But at length he said, "Go on then."

Not wanting to ask outright why Cait was so fretful, instead Ewan chose to ask the more apparent question. "Why has Cait never married?"

Silence hung in the air. Ewan could feel Matthew's sudden tension. After several moments passed, he muttered, "She's not ready."

Ewan canted his head to the side. "But...she's a woman grown."

"Even so, she is still not ready," Matthew shot back impatiently.

"Matthew, she is one and twenty," Ewan insisted, to which he received no answer, leaving him with no choice but to ask. "Then tell me this, why is she so fearful?"

"I do not wish to discuss that matter," Matthew said flatly.

But Ewan refused to be dismissed. "I remember hearing about some scandal that happened years ago..."

"I do not wish to discuss this," Matthew hissed.

Once again, Ewan drew his horse to a halt. When the clomping of Matthew's horse ceased, Ewan spoke, "Listen to me...for the first time in a long while I am thinking of someone else's pain other than my own, and it feels good. Tell me what truly happened to Cait all those years ago because I know she suffers."

"It doesn't concern ye," Matthew, his voice impassive.

"Matthew, I am not a stranger seeking idle gossip. She is dear to me and always has been. I never pried before because I assumed whatever happened was done and over. Tell me more. I want to help her if I can."

Matthew released a heavy sigh. "One of my brothers brought home a companion who tricked Cait into believing she was in love with him. They never exchanged vows, nor did he steal her maidenhood, but he did convince her to run away with him."

Ewan's blood ran cold. "My God, how old was ye?"

"Blast it all," Matthew snarled. "She was just ten and four, a child!"

Ewan's fists tightened around his reins. "The fiend! Can I assume ye or yer father has already robbed me of the pleasure of running him through?"

"Aye, he is dead, but not by my hand or anyone else's."

A fresh wave of dread entered Ewan's heart. "What happened?"

"He told her that we would never allow her to marry someone of humble birth. They stole away in the dead of night and set out for Largs where they boarded a ferry boat bound for Islay from which he hailed." As Matthew continued the anger fled his voice, leaving only heartache in its wake. "A storm struck the Firth of Clyde. Ye ken how merciless those waters are in autumn."

They rode in silence for some time. Ewan knew not to push his friend.

At length, Matthew continued. "Their ship overturned. I will not speak of what happened for I lack the strength to do so. In the end, Cait was the only survivor." As he continued his voice barely rose above a whisper. Ewan had to strain to hear his words over the rhythmic clomping of their horses' hooves. "The other passengers live on inside her. She hears their screams in her dreams." His voice broke. "I can't bear to picture her amidst the panic and death." Matthew took a deep breath. "She hears them even when she is awake. Seven years may have passed, but for her...'tis as if a part of her drowned alongside everyone else."

Ewan sat straight in his saddle. "But ye're wrong, Matthew."

"Be careful," Matthew growled. "I don't care if ye are blind, I will knock ye to the ground—"

"I'm not afraid of ye, nor will I allow ye to dismiss Cait's strength so readily."

"Trust me, Ewan. Ye cannot know the pain with which she lives."

Once again, Ewan drew his horse to a halt. "Moments ago, ye were telling me that time heals the wounds of the soul, yet by yer own words, ye've condemned Cait to death."

"Nay, that is not what I meant! Ye have to understand that the fear and suffering lives within her. She can't escape it. She—"

"Of course, she can't," Ewan said, interrupting. "Not when she's allowed to hide away in her chamber with her pain."

Silence hung between them as they rode on. At length, Matthew muttered, "Mayhap there is truth to yer words. Things were different then. My father was a hard, unforgiving man. It changed us all. I don't think any of us have ever forgiven ourselves for letting it happen in the first place. Mayhap, we do shelter her too much."

"Ye're not to blame, nor is yer father or yer brothers, and Cait was too young to be held accountable for her part. If she is ever to move on, she must forgive herself. And the rest of ye must forgive yerselves, too."

Now, Ewan understood why Cait was always so afraid. Better than most, he knew what it meant to be trapped in the dark.

Determination coursed through him as a new quest entered his heart.

He could no longer see the light, but he'd be damned if Cait could not.

"Let us return to the keep," he said to Matthew, reining in his horse once again.

"Wait," Matthew said and rested his hand on Ewan's arm. "Thank ye," he said quietly. "I'm glad ye've come."

"So am I," Ewan answered honestly.

There were three days until the lighting of the yule log. That evening, there would, no doubt, be a lively supper as everyone rested from the many preparations Ewan knew must be underway. A thrill of excitement shot through him. For the first time in a long while, he was looking forward to a night of festivity. He would make certain it was a joyful occasion for Cait, filled with laughter, and if he could figure out how to keep himself upright—he was determined to ask her to dance.

Chapter Six

Cait slowly meandered around her chamber, running a comb through her long black hair. Her heart thumped in her chest. Nerves certainly fueled her racing pulse, but something else brewed within her. At first, she could not name her emotion—so long had it been since she had felt it. But the quickening of her breath and her heart were not unpleasant.

In fact, it was thrilling.

It was...anticipation.

A smile came unbidden to her lips. She was filled with anticipation at the prospect of seeing Ewan again.

Closing her eyes, she imagined him standing with her, his long golden hair glinting in the fire light, his broad shoulders beckoning her touch, and his voice, deep and rich, soothing her heart like the notes of a gentle refrain.

Suddenly, she was struck by an impulse. Laying her comb on her bed, she closed her eyes and began to walk around her chamber, counting the steps from her bed to the chair by her hearth. Then she pivoted and crossed to her wardrobe, again counting the number of steps along the way. Her hand pressed her heart as a pang of sympathy sliced through her. How hard Ewan's life had become.

She longed to help him. The very idea gave her hope, not just for him, but for herself. If he could conquer the darkness and find new joy in his life, then mayhap so could she.

A knock sounded at the door.

"Enter," she called.

Helen appeared, carrying Cait's supper tray.

Taking a deep breath, Cait forced her spine poker straight. "I'm going to dine with my family in the great hall."

Helen's mouth dropped open an instant before a smile broke across her whole face. "My dear lady!" she exclaimed, but then she took a deep breath and cleared her throat. Turning away, she set down the tray. And when she turned back, she wore an impassive expression, but the glint in her eyes belied the calm tone to her voice as she casually asked, "Shall I help ye dress, my lady?"

Not waiting for Cait's answer, Helen crossed to the wardrobe and withdrew a deep blue tunic and a cream colored surcote with elaborate burgundy needlework.

Cait eyed the clothing nervously. "I do not wish to draw undue attention to myself."

Helen dismissed Cait's concern with a careless wave before pulling the tunic over Cait's head. "Ye wouldn't believe the mess Anna and Eleanor made of the kitchen just now," Helen began. "Water had to be brought to one of the chambers, but they had sent the kitchen lads off to fetch some jugs of wine from the buttery, which, by the by, Arlene had asked them to do. So, they had no choice but to carry the water themselves. Well, with buckets in hand, Anna was walking around one side of the table and Eleanor the other. Neither were looking at where they were going. I'm sure ye've guessed what happened next. And would ye believe the racket when they crashed together. Both useless, soppy messes on the floor, wailing about their sodden tunics and bruised backsides." Helen's voice was easy and unhurried, but also constant, barely stopping for breath.

Cait listened intently until Helen finished tying her surcote. Then her thoughts started to darken. Her fear rose to the fore of her mind.

"Nay, lass," Helen said, drawing her gaze. "Ye just keep listening to me while I dress yer hair." She led Cait to her chair and began to weave one side of her hair into a thick plait. "Ye can imagine that Arlene had a thing or two to say to them when she came in and found them wallowing on the floor in a puddle of water."

After Helen did the same to the other side of Cait's hair, she coiled the plaits together, weaving a crown on top of her head. Stepping back, Helen eyed her work. "I think we should leave off any coverings. Beauty such as yers needs no embellishment."

Cait blushed. "Surely ye exaggerate."

"Wheest," Helen said. "Enough of that, my lady."

Cait nodded, trying to seize her courage. Admiring the festive colors of her surcote, she smoothed her hands over the fabric, but then she faltered, feeling silly for allowing Helen to take extra time with her ablutions when Ewan wouldn't even be able to see her.

"My lady, look at me," Helen said, her voice firm. "Whatever it is ye're thinking right now—stop." Then her maid hastened across the room and opened her chamber door. "Now, walk with me, and listen to all I have to say."

Cait took a deep breath and nodded. Then she followed her maid out into the corridor. Helen commented on the candlelight and the freshly laid rushes as they walked. Cait tried to stay focused on Helen's humorous musings as they made their way through the keep.

When they reached the screen, beyond which lay the high dais, Helen turned about and faced Cait. "Now, how do ye feel?"

Cait took a deep breath. "Surprisingly well," she said truthfully.

Helen smiled. "Good. Now, don't think." She grabbed Cait by the shoulders, turned her about. "Just walk." Then she gave Cait a little shove forward. Stumbling into the open, Cait straightened, regaining her footing. Anna, clad in a fresh tunic, was filling her father's tankard. When the serving lass noticed Cait, a smile broke across her face. Anna cleared her throat. "My laird," she said and gestured discreetly to where Cait stood.

Her father twisted in his chair, and when he saw her, his face lit up. He pushed his chair back and stood. Then he crossed the high dais to greet her.

His silver eyes crinkled at the sides as he beamed at her. "What a happy surprise!"

On her father's arm, she approached the high table. Her brothers and Rowan stood and greeted her warmly. She smiled and bade them good evening, but her gaze kept darting back to the empty chair next to hers.

Ewan had not come down for supper.

Her chest tightened as she took her seat.

"I'm so glad ye've decided to join us," Lady Alana said. Then the older woman motioned to the empty chair between them. "Do ye mind?"

Cait forced a smile to her lips. "Of course not."

Lady Alana smiled brightly. She had delicate features and lovely green eyes. As she sat, her gaze searched Cait's face. "Are ye well?"

Cait nodded. "I am, thank ye." She straightened in her seat, determined to be a welcoming hostess. "Are ye enjoying yer stay?"

Lady Alana's face shone with enthusiasm. "Indeed. Yer keep is beautiful." But her easy countenance suddenly vanished. She leaned close and in a low voice said, "I have been waiting for a chance to speak with ye." She took a deep breath. "I want to apologize for what happened the other evening. Ewan is not himself."

Cait shook her head. "Ye needn't apologize. Neither ye nor Laird MacLeod has done anything wrong."

A sad smile curved her lips. "'Tis gracious of ye to say as much." Her straight spine softened, and she breathed out a tired sigh. "Still, my heart is sorry..." Her gaze dropped and her voice grew distant. "I'm sorry for him, for my people."

Cait felt Lady Alana's heartache so acutely. She reached out and gently squeezed the older woman's hand.

The caring gesture filled Lady Alana's face with warmth as she, once more, met Cait's gaze. "Do ye remember Ewan from his stay here all those years ago?"

Cait nodded. "How could I not? I was very fond of him."

"I wish ye'd had the chance to meet him again as a woman grown. What a man he was," she said wistfully.

"He is still the same man," Cait offered in a soft voice.

Lady Alana nodded. "I ken ye're right. 'Tis what I believe as does Rowan and our people." She lifted her shoulders. "Regrettably, he does not, even though he has regained much of the strength his fever stole. And if ye could only know how hard he has labored to be independent. He can move about Castle Laoch entirely on his own. And allowing he has a companion to ensure his path is clear, he walks through our village with ease." Her gaze filled with pride. "He counts the steps and knows how many strides from the keep to the front gate and the front gate to the outer wall." But as she continued, her smile faltered. "I've tried to celebrate these victories with him, but he only shakes his head and says something about how a laird must be able to do more than find his own way to his chamber." Tears flooded her eyes. "Sometimes, I fear that mayhap he is right—"

"Nay," Cait blurted, hearing the doubt in Lady Alana's voice. "Do not lose faith in him, my lady."

Eyes wide, Lady Alana's hand fluttered to her heart. "I was...wasn't I?"

Cait looked her straight on. "Ye must stay strong."

Ewan's mother took a deep breath and squared her shoulders. "Ye're right. After all, I am asking him to not surrender, to keep fighting. How can he if I falter?"

"Never lose faith, my lady," Cait insisted. "Still, ye must also remember to be gentle with yerself."

Lady Alana leaned close and pressed a kiss to Cait's cheek. "Thank ye."

Cait's heart swelled and she straightened in her seat. Not only had she and Lady Alana conversed with ease, but Cait had also soothed and encouraged the older woman.

"My lady."

Both Cait and Lady Alana looked up. Matthew stood in front of them. He bowed to Ewan's mother. "Would ye like to join in the dancing?"

Lady Alana shifted her gaze to Cait. "Suddenly, I do feel like dancing." Turning back to Matthew, she dipped her head. "I would love to."

Cait watched as Matthew and Lady Alana joined hands with her kin who were circling around the trestle tables, skipping and kicking up their heels. She glanced sidelong at the empty chair next to hers, and then the image of Ewan sitting alone in his chamber came to the fore of her thoughts. How she longed to see him, but it wouldn't be proper for her to call on him in his room without reason. Then she straightened, suddenly filled with new hope—mayhap someone still needed to bring up his tray.

"Cait," her father said, drawing her gaze. "Do ye also wish to join the dance?"

"If ye don't mind, I think I will retire now," she said. Her conscience pricked at lying to her father, but she could not bring herself to admit how much she wanted to see Ewan again.

Argyle patted her hand lovingly. "Ye've done well tonight, lass. I'm proud of ye."

She pushed her chair back and stood. Then, she bent at the waist and kissed her father's whiskered cheek. "I love ye, Da."

Turning away, her breath hitched as she nearly walked straight into the very person she had been longing to see. "Forgive me," she gasped. "I didn't see ye there."

Ewan smiled, making her knees weak. "I didn't see ye either."

Laughter fled her lips, and she craned her neck back to take in the rugged lines of his jaw and his full, sensual lips. His golden hair shone in the candlelight as did his bronzed skin that peeked out from the deep V of his tunic. She licked her lips that had suddenly gone dry. "I'm glad ye've come."

He dipped his head to her. "Please forgive my late arrival. I was overdue for a wash, and some of yer servants ran into a little trouble when they were fetching the water, or so I was told." He smiled. "If I heard the story correctly, the trouble they ran into was each other."

Remembering the story Helen had just told her about Anna and Eleanor sprawled out on the kitchen floor in a puddle, she laughed outright.

His face beamed down at her. "Yer laughter is a sound I wish to hear for the rest of the evening." His voice softened. "For the rest of forever, actually."

Her breath caught as he touched her arm and traced the length to her hand, which he clasped and brought to his lips. She swallowed hard, her heart, suddenly, thumping in her chest.

He canted his head to the side. "Judging by the lively pipers and rhythmic clomping on the stone floor, I can only assume yer clan has begun a festive reel."

She smiled. "Indeed, they have."

He stepped back and bowed. Then he offered her his hand. "Would ye care to join?" The corner of his mouth lifted in a sideways smile that made her legs trembled. "That is, allowing ye can lead me safely down the stairs to the main floor."

She chuckled. "I will try," she said. "But I warn ye, my legs feel like porridge."

"I'm certain that ye're mistaken, although I think yer brothers would pummel me to the ground if I lifted yer skirts to prove ye wrong."

Her laughter rang out.

His smile widened in approval. "Ye have the most beautiful laugh."

His strong warrior's hand clasped hers, fueling her strength as she led him toward the stairwell. "We've reached the first step," she said. "There are seven."

Together, they descended, reaching the last step just as a group of dancers skipped toward them. "Are we going to join with the others?" she asked.

He shook his head. "I'm liable to fall flat on my face. But I can hold yer hands, and we can make our own circle." He drew close and outstretched his other hand. Her heart raced faster as she slid her hand in his. "Here we go," he blurted. "Let me know if we're about to dance into something." Then, he twirled her in a circle. "How am I doing thus far?" he asked playfully.

"We're both still standing," she laughed.

His laughter, deep and rich, rang out. "To the left," he called. But they moved in opposite directions, jerking one another. Laughing again, he called. "I meant to yer left."

They sashayed from left to right, and then, once again, he led her in a circle, all the while making her laugh until she could barely draw breath. Her gaze never left his face, which shone with rugged vitality.

When the music ended, the room erupted into cheers. She jumped a little at the sound. Scanning the great room, she saw that everyone's attention was on her and Ewan. Her face burned.

"Thank ye, Cait," Ewan said, drawing her gaze. Then he dropped her hand, and he too began to clap. "Aye, Clan Campbell has fine musicians, and are, indeed, worthy of such praise!"

Breathless, her heart racing, she leaned close and whispered in his ear. "My people are not cheering for the musicians. They cheer for us."

His brows shot wide for a moment. "Do yer father and brothers join in the celebration or do they look as if they want to beat me nigh to death?"

She glanced up at the high table. "Our families are smiling."

He breathed out a rush of air. "That's a relief. I'm not as accurate with my fists as I once was." He paused for a moment, but then he cleared his throat. "Follow my lead." A smile broke across his face, and he bowed at the waist, causing her people to cheer all the more. Breathless, she, too, smiled and dipped in a quick curtsy.

Squeezing her hand, he leaned close and asked, "Can I assume ye wish to be anywhere but here at this moment?"

"Aye," she said quickly.

He dropped her hand and offered her his arm. "Shall we?"

She wove her arm through his. "Where am I taking us?"

"I would suggest to the nearest way out."

"This way, then," she breathed as she led him toward the closest door, which was the servant's entrance to the kitchen. When they passed through the door, the cheering died down and the musicians struck up another lively song. Holding his hand, they wound through the kitchen, exchanging good wishes with the servants they passed along the way. Finally, they reached the stairwell that led to the upper rooms. When they stepped onto the landing, she stopped. "My heart is pounding," she said, breathlessly. "And my legs feel like they are about to give out."

"Are we alone?" he asked.

She nodded, and then remembered to reply. "Aye."

Before she knew what was happening, he swept her into his arms, cradling her. "Lead me to yer chamber."

Lured by his masculine scent and hard physique, she melted into his warmth and rested her head against his strong chest. "Turn to yer right," she bade him softly. "Then carry on straight."

Candlelight illuminated the corridor. "We have reached yer chamber," she told him.

A frown shaped his brow. He set her feet on the floor and reached out, running his hand down the slatted wood door. Then he turned to her with a questioning look on his face. "I had meant to escort ye to yer chamber."

"And so ye are," she said as she took his hand and began to lead him forward, counting the steps in her head. She stopped at the foot of her stairwell. "These stairs circle around and lead to my chamber. I counted ten and eight strides."

His breath caught. He squatted down and began hastily running his hands down the wall and then across the first steps. "Cait," he called out.

She stepped forward and took his hand. "I'm here."

He stood. "'Tis ye," he rasped, clasping her hand to his chest. She could feel his heart pounding. Tears flooded his amber gaze. "Ye're the piper!"

HIS HAND SHOOK AS HE reached out, searching for her cheek. When his fingers grazed her skin, she cupped his hand, pressing her cheek into his palm.

"I can't believe 'tis ye." His heart swelled. "I've listened to ye play every night since we arrived. I...I cannot tell ye how much yer music has meant to me." His hand dropped to her waist as he pulled her close. He felt her tremble in his arms. "When I first arrived, I felt so alone, and..." He swallowed hard, seizing his courage to utter the words in his heart. "And afraid. But yer music...yer music has been a candle in the dark."

Her arms encircled his neck. "I did not know anyone could hear me," she whispered, her voice tremulous.

He drew away slightly and softly ran his fingers down her cheek. He felt her tears, and again, he held her close. "Dear Cait, please don't cry," he crooned. "I wish to make ye laugh, to make ye happy."

"But ye have made me happy," she said in a rush. "Knowing my music has touched yer heart the same way it fills my own..." Her voice broke. "'Tis the greatest joy I've ever known."

He crushed her close, his soul replete with her in his arms. "I hate to let ye go," he whispered.

"Then don't," she replied, making his heart soar.

His hold tightened around her feminine curves. He breathed deep the lavender scent of her hair, but then he did what he knew he must and slowly released her. His hands ached to hold her again, but he forced himself to step back. "Good night, fair Cait."

"Good night, Ewan." Her hand slowly coursed down his arm. He savored her lingering touch. "Thank ye for the dance," she whispered.

His heart thumped in his chest as he waited at the foot of the stairs and listened to her footfalls circle around. She climbed so high that he realized her chamber must have been the tower room that was built straight out from the keep, soaring above the other towers. He smiled to himself, imagining her sitting near the casement, staring out at the world below.

With a full heart, he slowly retreated to his chamber. Crossing the room, he sat on the edge of his bed and unlaced his brogues. Then he slid the top of his plaid down his shoulder and pulled his tunic over his head. He was about to unbuckle his belt when the first notes reached his ears. His heart swelled. Not waiting to finish undressing, he lay back on the bed and closed his eyes and let Cait's music caress his very soul.

A smile curved his lips knowing that she played for him.

With her silken message blanketing his heart, he could almost feel her in his arms as he drifted off to sleep.

EWAN SAT UP WITH A start. His heart pounded in his ears while a sense of foreboding weighed heavily on his chest. Something had awoken him. Holding his breath, he lay still while he listened for movement. Hearing nothing, he sat up and swung his legs over the side of the bed and reached for his sword.

"Is anyone there?"

He listened intently, but silence was the only reply. His shoulders eased slightly as he leaned his sword back against the wall. Expelling a long breath, he rested his head in his hands, willing the tightness in his chest to release.

But then he stiffened when he heard a faint cry.

Sitting straight, he held his breath and listened. A moment later, a scream pierced his heart.

"Cait!" He stood and charged across the room and threw open the door. Dragging his hand across the wall, he hastened down the corridor. Again, a mournful cry reached his ears. He did not hesitate when he reached her stairwell. Winding around and around, he ascended the tall tower, and when the stairs ended, he held his arms out and moved forward until he connected with the slatted wood of her door. Finding the handle, he threw it open and barreled into the room, hastening toward the sounds of her distress. His legs struck the side of her bed. "Cait," he said, reaching out. He could feel her trembling, as she muttered something indiscernible, and he realized she was dreaming. "Wake up, Cait!" He gathered her in his arms.

Her breath hitched and her arms came around his neck. "Ewan," she cried, and she crumpled in his arms. She shook with sobs, her arms squeezing him tightly. The sound of her heartache struck him to his core. He wanted nothing more in that moment than to ease her suffering forever. Rocking her gently, he crooned softly in her ears. "Ye're safe, lass. I've got ye."

She melted against him. The contours of her body curved softly in his arms. Shudders of pain racked her shoulders, but after a while, the rawness of her sobs began to ease into gentle tears. And when, at last, her tears were spent, still he held her close, surrounding her, shielding her. "Ye are safe, Cait. I will never let anything happen to ye."

"But it already has happened," she said in a weak voice. "And no matter how much time passes, I cannot escape that day."

"Ye can. I know ye can, and I'm going to help ye," he vowed.

Still, she shook. He could feel her struggle with her fear, raw and immediate after her nightmare. "Ye can't save me, Ewan. No one can. I'm alone in the dark."

He cupped her cheeks. "Then I will hold ye in the dark and in the light. Ye're not alone, Cait, not anymore."

A fresh sob tore from her throat as she threw her arms around his neck. Again, he rocked her, holding her close. He pressed soft kisses to her hair and stroked her back. "I'm here with ye," he crooned. "Ye're not alone."

After a while, her trembling ceased. She gently pulled away, moving to sit beside him on her bed.

Silence hung in the air.

"I cannot see yer face to read yer thoughts," he said. "Speak to me."

She reached out and took his hand. "I'm embarrassed," she whispered.

"Och, lass." He wrapped his arm around her waist. "Please, don't be," he whispered back. "I know what it is to feel hopeless..." He cupped her cheek. "But then I came here. And do ye know what I found?"

"Nay," she whispered.

"Hope...I found hope in ye."

"That's not possible," she murmured.

"But it is, Cait. And now I know two truths." His hand traveled back down her arm, and he took her hand and pressed it to his chest. "The first is that our wounds can heal. I understand that now, but the second is that the scars will always remain. Like the pot, remember?"

"Aye," she said, and he could hear the smile in her voice. "Dented, not broken."

Just then the chapel bell tolled for *Lauds*.

Ewan stiffened. "*Prime* will soon be upon us. I should go. As good a friend as I am to Matthew, he would not take kindly to finding me in yer chamber whilst ye're wearing nothing but yer chemise."

She inhaled sharply, and he felt her fumble for a blanket, which he didn't doubt she was using to cover herself. He flashed her a smile. "Ye needn't fash yerself, lass. I didn't see anything."

Gentle laughter reached his ears and his heart swelled. "'Tis glad I am to hear ye laugh."

"I seem to do that quite often in yer company."

He stood then. "I will need yer help finding yer chamber door."

"Of course," she said.

When she took hold of his hand, it was all he could do not to pull her close and wrap her in his arms. He wanted to kiss her full lips until the world melted away and all that remained was each other.

"This way," she said.

When they reached her chamber door, she asked, "Shall I lead ye downstairs?"

He shook his head. "Nay, I know the way." He hesitated at the door. "Cait, I meant what I said about finding hope since coming here. I would like to stay for a while, and get to know ye better; that is, if ye wish it of me."

For a moment, silence was his only reply. But then her hands came to rest on his shoulders. She drew close so that he could feel her warm breath on his bare chest. Then her soft lips pressed against his cheek, gently stoking the desire that set his body aflame.

"I would like that very much," she whispered.

A slow smile stretched across his face as he savored her touch. "Good morrow, fair Cait," he beamed.

"Good morrow, Ewan. It has been a long time since I said that and actually meant it. Thank ye."

"For what?"

"For coming to Castle Shéan."

He dipped his head to her before he began his slow descent. As he wound down the stairwell, joy pulsed through him. And it occurred to him that only days before he'd been reluctant to enter Castle Shéan, and now...he knew he'd never want to leave.

Chapter Seven

Cait's gaze remained fixed on Ewan as he slowly stepped down the stairs. The top folds of his plaid hung loosely over his belt, and he wore no shirt, allowing her gaze to feast upon his broad shoulders and the muscles shifting in his back as he descended. His strong hand dragged the wall, which she knew he did to keep his bearings. When he disappeared from view, she was immediately struck by a longing so great that it made her chest ache.

Closing the door, she rested her back against it and expelled a long, wistful breath. Her heart raced. Her stomach fluttered, and she couldn't have stopped smiling if she tried. Closing her eyes, she remembered her suffering when she had first awoken. She had been drowning in the same misery that had been slowly choking the life from her body for years, and then, suddenly, he was there, holding her, telling her everything was going to be all right. And for the first time since a family of fishermen found her washed upon the shores of the Isle of Arran, she believed she could, indeed, find peace.

Her mind was racing, but her thoughts did not torment her with fierce storms and piercing screams. For so long, she had made her life small as she feared to move beyond the shield of her father and brothers' strength. But having witnessed Ewan's struggle to rise above his own dark fate, she knew that she, too, could have more....be more, just as Helen and Arlene had always told her. All she needed to do was believe in herself.

She crossed to the bed and spread her arms and legs wide and fell onto her back.

Once again, she felt Ewan's strong arms surround her. Her heart swelled with feelings she had long thought dead—love, hope, joy, and the sheer excitement of knowing that anything was possible.

Sitting up, she walked with determination to her wardrobe and reached for a tunic, which she quickly pulled over her head. Then she put her arms through the sleeves of a surcote, but she struggled to tie the laces. And then suddenly, she thought of her sister-in-law, Tempest, who was sister to Elora—her brother Nathan's wife.

Both their families had said that Cait and Tempest resembled each other so much in appearance that they could be twins. Both had long raven black hair and deep blue eyes, and even their features were similar, both having wide mouths with full lips and pert, upturned noses. But appearances aside, they could not have been more different.

Tempest was fearless—some even thought her reckless. She never wore a surcote or plaited her hair. She moved through life as confident as any maid ever had.

Wanting to push herself to be bold, Cait said aloud, "What would Tempest do?"

With a deep breath, she pulled her surcote off and hung it back on its peg. Then she seized a belt, which she tied loosely, letting it rest low on her hips. Running her fingers through her hair, she smoothed out the tangles, then swept her long, black waves off her shoulders. A nervous laugh burst from her lips as she spun in a circle. She hadn't dressed in such simple garb since she was a wee lass.

Taking up her pipe, she crossed the room to her casement and opened the shutters. The crisp winter air sent a shiver up her spine, but despite the cold, she leaned out. The village unfolded before her. Her gaze traced the ribbon of road from the outer walls of Castle Shéan through the clusters of thatched homes, then over the snow swept moorland in the distance. Bringing her pipe to her lips, she blew her joy into the notes that flowed out of her brightly. Instead of a mournful refrain, her fingers moved in new patterns, creating a lively tune to which lovers might dance. All the while, she waited, a part of her quietly counting the moments until the chapel bell ushered in the hour of *Prime*.

When, at last, the first chime rang out, she set her pipe down and drew her shutters closed. Then, sliding her feet into a pair of soft leather slippers, she swung open her door and started down the stairs humming quietly to herself to keep her thoughts from betraying her newfound resolve.

As she passed Ewan's chamber door, she paused and pressed her hand to the slatted wood. Her heart fluttered with excitement at the prospect of seeing him again. Hastening down the corridor, she headed straight for the great hall where she knew Ewan would eventually join her. Together, with their families at their sides, they would break their fast. But as she neared the solar, she heard her father's voice.

"Cait is a very special young woman. I'm not certain marriage is the right choice for her."

Her heart started to pound as she tiptoed closer to the solar door, which was partially ajar.

"I love her," she heard Ewan say.

She pressed her hand over her mouth to silence her hitching breath.

"I know we have only just become reacquainted after so many years apart, but, Argyle, I do love her. And I feel certain she cares for me."

Cait beamed. Ewan loved her. She threw her head back and flung her arms out to the side as she silently savored his declaration.

"I do not doubt the truth of yer feelings, but..." her father's words trailed off. His disparaging tone made her falter.

"Argyle, I mean this with every due respect, but Cait is stronger than ye realize."

Her heart leapt when she heard Ewan defend her strength.

Her father blew out a long breath. "But to marry ye, she must leave Castle Shéan. How can I ask her to do that when she barely leaves her own chamber?"

Suddenly, her stomach dropped out. Her father was right. If she were to marry Ewan, she would be Lady of Castle Laoch. Her chest tightened. She could feel her fear rise to the surface, but she clenched her fists, holding fast to her calm. In that moment, she knew she had just arrived at a crossroads. One path led to a lifetime of seclusion and sorrow, and the other to healing and love.

Tossing her unbound hair over her shoulder, she stood tall. She had already made her choice.

She chose hope.

Eager to tell her father just that, she raised her hand to rap on the door but faltered when Ewan next spoke.

"She doesn't have to leave Castle Shéan; that is, if ye will welcome me here to stay."

Her father chuckled. "I appreciate yer eagerness to make my daughter feel comfortable, but ye'll find it hard to lead yer people from here."

"That will not be a problem as I am giving up the chiefdom."

Her chest tightened. Why would he do that? Backing away from the door, her heart started to race. Did he not think her capable of being lady to his people? Despite his earlier defense of her strength, clearly, he didn't believe she was actually ready to move on. Tears stung her eyes. She gripped her chest, feeling as if he had sunk a knife into her heart.

"I wish for yer daughter and I to be betrothed with a nonbinding contract. That way, she can take whatever time she needs, and I can settle into life here at Castle Shéan. This will also allow my brother time to adjust to his new responsibilities as laird."

"Ewan, I think ye're making a grave mistake by relinquishing the chiefdom," Argyle said, voicing his disapproval. "But if Matthew, Rowan, and yer mother have been unable to sway ye from this course, I'm not arrogant enough to believe there is anything I could say to ye that would make a difference." Again, her father sighed. "Yer feelings for Cait are genuine, this I do not doubt."

"I need her, Argyle. She is all goodness and light," Ewan insisted.

Nay, she longed to shout. *Ye do not see my light, not really!*

Thunder suddenly shuddered through her, followed by a piercing scream that she knew only she could hear. Taking several more steps back, she could feel herself begin to unravel.

Heart pounding, she hastened down the hallway, trying to out-run the assault pummeling her mind.

"Stop it," she cried, begging the storm to pass.

She stumbled on the hem of her tunic as she wound around her narrow stairwell until, at last, she reached her chamber. A sob tore from her throat as she lunged for her pipe. Fingers trembling, she blew her heartache into song. She felt like she was spiraling into herself, growing smaller and smaller. Finally, all that remained was the mournful lament of her pipe. The music dispersed the storm clouds from her mind, leaving a black sky in its wake, studded with amber stars, which snuffed out one by one with each heart-rending note she played.

EWAN LEFT THE SOLAR with Argyle's blessing echoing in his mind. Warmth radiated throughout his body. His smile could not be contained as he dragged his fingers along the wall to ensure he did not lose his way.

"Good morrow, Laird MacLeod," a young woman said.

"Ewan will do, thank ye," he said brightly.

"'Tis Anna, Lair...er...Ewan. I brought ye yer supper tray a few evenings past."

"Good morrow, Anna," he said, resisting the sudden urge to hug her, so great was his happiness.

"Can I help ye to yer chamber, Ewan?"

"I know my way, Anna, but thank ye, and many Yuletide blessings, for ye and yer family."

"Thank ye, and the same to ye Laird MacLeo—I mean, Ewan!"

As he continued down the corridor his heart raced, drumming in his chest. He felt stronger and more vital than he had in months. And for the first time since tragedy had laid him low, his life suddenly had promise and purpose. He could not wait to tell Cait the good news.

When he at last climbed to the top of her tower, he rapped on the door. "Cait, 'tis Ewan," he called out in his excitement. The sound of his pounding heart hammered in his ears as he waited for her to open the door. At last, he heard the hinges creak.

"Cait!" he beamed.

"What is it?" she answered, her voice oddly flat.

His brow furrowed with concern. "Is something the matter?"

"I'm not feeling well," she murmured.

"I have news that might help." He held out his hands, but she did not reach for him. "Come to me, Cait. Take my hands." He waited, his pulse racing as his chest tightened against a sudden foreboding that wished to steal his newfound bliss. He released his breath in a rush when, at last, her hands clasped his.

"Ye're freezing," he exclaimed and pressed her hands to his chest. "No matter, I shall warm them." Smiling, he pulled her close. "Ye shall never be cold or lonely or sorrowful ever again, for I have spoken with yer father. He has consented to a betrothal...that is, if ye'll have me." He swallowed hard. As moments passed and she did not reply, he could no longer ignore how stiff she felt in his arms. His smile faltered. He had assumed that Cait's response would mirror his own. His full heart longed for her to throw her arms around his neck and gleefully shout her acceptance for all the world to hear.

"Cait?" he asked as a hollowness settled in his chest.

"I'm not ready," she whispered.

"Nay," he said, his hands gripping her shoulders. "Ye are. I know ye are. And ye needn't be afraid. We can stay here at Castle Shéan. It will be just the two of us—"

"What about yer home? Ye're Laird of Clan Macleod."

"But that's just it," he said, once more allowing hope to enter his heart. "There is nothing standing in our way. I am relinquishing the chiefdom to Rowan."

She pulled free from his embrace. "Ye think so little of me that ye'd rather give up yer title than have me sit as Lady of Castle Laoch."

The pit of his stomach dropped out. "What are ye talking about?"

"Why else would ye stand down?"

He took a step back. "I have sought to convince my stubborn brother to take on the role long before I came here. He must. 'Tis his duty."

"Why must he?" she demanded.

He raked his hand through his hair. "I thought that ye of all people would understand."

"Why must Rowan be laird?"

He shook his head, not believing that he was having to defend his choice to her. "Because, Cait, if ye hadn't noticed, I'm blind."

"That doesn't mean ye must surrender the chiefdom."

His body tensed. "What do ye know about it? I thought ye wanted to be together, to heal our dented souls, or was that talk about pots just rubbish?"

"Ewan, if ye give up yer title and leave yer people, we are not healing together—we're hiding." Her voice broke. "I don't want to hide anymore!"

He threw his hands ups. "Cait, what do ye want from me? I cannot lead my people like this." His fists clenched together. "I am blind," he growled.

"Aye," she said. The bitterness of her tone cut straight through his heart. "Ye are blind."

Feeling as if his head was on fire, Ewan stumbled toward the door. Circling around and around, he retreated from her castle tower on limbs that shook, threatening to give way. He could barely draw breath as he hastened toward his chamber. Gasping and shaking, he retrieved his cloak from his wardrobe. Without a thought or care for the rest of his belongings, he left his room behind. Following the corridor to its end, he turned away from the passage that would eventually lead past the solar and out on the high dais and went the other way. He knew there was bound to be a servant's passage that would take him to the lower level of the keep without running into his family or any well-meaning Campbell.

"Ewan," a familiar voice said.

He jerked around. "Timothy, is that ye?"

"Aye," the lad said, drawing close. "I think ye got a bit turned around. The passage to the solar and great hall is back the other way."

Ewan hastened toward him. "I need ye to lead me the stables," he said in a rush. "But ye mustn't allow anyone to see us. Do ye understand, Timothy?"

"I will try," the lad answered.

"That is not good enough," Ewan hissed. "I need yer word."

After a moment's pause, Timothy vowed, "Ye have my word, no one will see us."

Expelling a rush of air, Ewan reached out. "May I rest my hand on yer shoulder."

"Of course," Timothy replied.

Feeling the lad's surprising strength beneath his fingers, he urged him forward. "Just get me out of here," he gasped, feeling as if he were suffocating.

"This way," Timothy said, his voice strong.

Ewan lost track of the turns and stairs, allowing himself to be led by the young lad like a ship adrift on the waves. More than once, he pulled Ewan to the side, telling him to be still while footfalls hastened past. Finally, the smell of horses and fresh cut hay reached his nose.

"Lead me to my horse's stall."

"Here he is," Timothy said. "And a beauty to be sure."

Ewan reached out and drew a deep breath when he felt his mount's sinewy strength. Slowly, he exhaled and rested his cheek against his horse's muzzle.

"Is there anything else I can do?" Timothy asked.

Ewan nodded and murmured, "Find the captain of my guard. Tell him to join me here straightaway."

Ewan listened to Timothy's footfalls scamper from the stables. In the quiet of the moment, the weight of his last exchange with Cait descended upon him. Her last bitter words echoed again and again in his mind.

Ye are blind.

"Nay," he growled aloud against the pain.

In response, his horse snorted and tossed his head.

"'Tis all right," Ewan crooned, soothing a hand down his mount's neck. He forced his mind to listen to the sounds around him, the snorting beasts and clomping hooves, hollowing out his aching heart.

Hurried footsteps pricked his ear. He straightened, turning his face toward the sound.

"My laird," his captain said. "What is yer will?"

The sound of Andrew's voice strengthened Ewan's resolve. "To leave Castle Shéan straightaway."

"But, my laird, tomorrow is Yule. Why—"

"I gave ye an order," Ewan snapped. "We leave immediately."

"If that is yer will, my laird, I will gather the men and alert yer brother and mother to yer wishes."

"Nay," he hissed. "Ye and I will take our leave. The other men will escort my family when they choose to depart."

A long pause followed. "Ye wish to strike out alone?"

Ewan simply nodded his answer.

Andrew cleared his throat. "If that is yer will, then I will go to the keep and tell yer brother—"

"Nay," Ewan interrupted. "Timothy shall bring them a message. Timothy, are ye here?"

"Aye, Ewan."

"Come closer."

"I'm here," Timothy said.

Ewan reached out and found Timothy's shoulder. "Thank ye for yer service. Ye're a good lad." Intent on clasping Timothy's hand, Ewan's own hand moved down the lad's arm when suddenly his flesh turned hard and cold. "What's this?"

"'Tis my arm," Timothy answered simply.

"What happened to the arm ye were born with? The one made of flesh and blood."

"God needed another hand to do his good works, or at least that's what my mum told me."

"Do ye mean to say that ye were born with only one arm?"

"Indeed, I was."

Ewan frowned. "But I thought ye told me ye were going to begin an apprenticeship with the smithy."

"I am," Timothy said proudly. "I begin in the new year."

Ewan's frown deepened. "But ye only have one arm."

"Nay, Ewan, I have two. The one God gave me, and the one the smithy fashioned for me. 'Tis made of iron and leather."

"Isn't the smithy worried that ye won't be able to learn the trade?"

"Why would he? My mind is sound."

"Ye're a keen lad to be sure," Ewan assured him. "What I meant to say is wouldn't another lad be more capable of the job?"

Timothy snorted. "When I was small, some would try to tell me I was different, that I would never be like the other lads. But that never stopped me." Ewan could almost see Timothy's chest puff out with pride. "The smithy's chosen me because I'm the strongest and hardest working lad in the village."

Ewan shook his head in amazement. "Ye sound as if ye're glad ye were born this way."

"I wasn't always, but we all must accept who we are and make the best of it. I mean, what would ye do if someone tried to tell ye that ye weren't capable of being laird anymore?"

Ewan's chest tightened. "I...I'm not sure."

"I'll tell ye what ye'd do. Ye'd say that ye were the finest swordsman in the Highlands, and that ye lost yer sight defending yer people's lives. Then ye'd call out whomever slandered ye and demand to know whether they had made a sacrifice as great. I'd wager their tongues would stop wagging soon enough."

Ewan turned his back to the lad as a knot formed in his throat. In that moment, the weight of his bitterness descended on him, bringing him to his knees. He gripped his head with his hands as rage and grief surged upward from deep within his soul. He roared aloud, releasing his pain. It poured out of him, all his shame, all his fear.

Then he slumped over, weak...empty.

Nothing remained but for the memory of a single breathless note of music that coiled around his bleeding heart—the quiet memory of a piper's song that had sparked his first glimpse of hope.

In that one note, he found her again—Cait, in all her glory and vulnerability.

Within her gaze, he could see himself as she did—strong, gentle, and perfectly flawed. And then he realized the simplest truth of all—that he was enough.

He was Laird Ewan MacLeod, and he was enough.

"My laird, what is wrong?" Andrew asked quietly.

Lifting his head high, Ewan stood, rising tall. Then he turned around and faced his captain. "Nothing," he replied, releasing a long breath. "There is nothing wrong with me."

After several moments passed, Andrew asked, "What is yer will? Do ye still wish to leave?"

"Aye," Ewan said, determination filling his stance. "But gather the rest of the men. We ride out together."

"But what of yer family?"

"Just trust me," Ewan said. "Trust me as ye have always done."

"Aye, my laird."

Ewan listened to the captain's retreating footsteps. Then he turned to Timothy. "Will ye help me saddle my horse."

"Of course," the lad replied.

BEFORE TOO LONG, EWAN sat astride his horse, along with half a dozen MacLeod warriors. "Timothy," he called.

"I'm here."

"Will ye ride with me?"

"I cannot go as far as MacLeod territory, but I will join ye for a spell."

Ewan smiled and reached his hand down. His fingers closed around cold metal. He swung the lad up behind him. "We're not riding to Castle Laoch." Then, he said to Timothy, "Be my eyes. Tell me when only the tallest tower of Castle Shéan can be seen."

The thunder of hooves surrounded him as he galloped forward. The crisp winter wind cut through the fabric of his cloak and tunic, but he welcomed the exhilaration of the icy breeze.

After a short while, Timothy said behind him, his voice raised to carry over the din of the horses' hooves, "Ewan, I can no longer see the tower."

Ewan jerked his horse to a halt. When the rest of his men had reined in their mounts, he turned his own around so that he faced them. "Warriors of Clan MacLeod," he called out. "For months now, I have failed ye. But not because of a weakness of the body, for which I have placed all blame, but rather a weakness in my soul," he slammed his fist to his chest. "But no more," he called louder. "I will rise up for ye, for the people of Clan MacLeod. I will rise up for myself, and I will never surrender to fear again. Hold fast," he shouted, sounding the motto of his people.

"Hold fast," his men bellowed in reply.

Hearing his men cheer, his heart filled as never before. "Warriors of Clan MacLeod, I cannot give these stolen months back to ye, but I can give ye back the dignity of our name. Captain," he called.

"Aye, my laird," Andrew said, his voice reverent.

"Erect the banners of our people! Raise the crest of the MacLeod!"

"Aye, my laird!"

"And Captain, send a rider ahead to Castle Shéan."

"But we just left the keep and village behind. What message could ye need to send?"

"We came here under a blanket of my shame. I would give my men the welcome of which they were robbed by my own hand. Ride now, back to Castle Shéan. Tell them to prepare for the coming of the warriors and the Chieftain of Clan Macleod!"

Chapter Eight

Cait sat in a chair near her open casement, wrapped in a blanket as she gazed out over the frost covered hills. In that moment, all she wanted was to go back to the night before when she had been cradled in Ewan's arms and felt new hope enter her soul. Now, a fresh pain gripped her heart. Still, despite her sorrow, she knew that something had happened to her, something irrevocable.

She had felt her own strength. She had faced her fears and stood her ground, and now, she could no longer doubt herself.

The thunder of hooves reached her ears. She straightened in her seat to look down at the distant courtyard below. Half a dozen MacLeod warriors were leaving the castle on horseback. Holding her breath, she scanned the men. Then her gaze settled on broad shoulders and golden hair.

She gripped the window ledge. Surely, he wasn't leaving. How could he? Not while there was still so much left unsaid. Had he lost all hope?

"Come back," she muttered. Her heart pounded in her ears as she watched him crest over distant hills, and then he was gone.

"Nay," she cried, gripping her chest. She slumped back in her chair. Tears coursed down her cheeks as she lay her head back and gazed up at the austere white sky. Fighting to breathe, she gripped the arms of her chair, and for a moment, she knew only despair. But then she forced herself to sit up. She knew the darkness that clawed at her feet, fighting to pull her beneath bleak waves.

"Nay," she said out loud as she stood. Just then, a knock sounded at the door, and a moment later, Matthew entered the room.

They locked eyes. His brows drew together. "Ye saw him leave, didn't ye?" he asked softly.

Her face crumpled. He was at her side an instant later. He scooped her into his arms and carried her to the edge of the bed. Gently, he rocked her, and pressed a kiss to her temple.

"Cait, I'm so sorry," he crooned. "This is all my fault. Had I not insisted Ewan come, then none of this would have happened."

Cait jerked upright and swiped at her cheeks. "I do not regret his coming. I'm heartsore right now, but, in time, my heart will mend. And when it does, I'll be ready."

He gave her a curious look. "Ready for what?"

She lifted her shoulders. "For whatever life holds for me, I suppose." She freed herself from Matthew's embrace. "I'm done hiding. I just wish..." Her voice broke. "I just wish Ewan was ready, too."

Matthew smiled despite her tears. "Ye're an amazing woman, Cait."

Seeing the admiration in her warrior brother's face, fueled her courage to new heights. Willing her heart to fill, despite the hollowness in her chest, she tossed her hair over her shoulder. "Please tell our father that the Lady of Castle Shéan will be attending this evening's feast." Her voice was tremulous, but her resolve was steadfast.

Matthew beamed at her. A slight smile curved his lips as he lifted her feet off the ground and hugged her with all his might. When he set her feet down, a knock sounded at the door.

"Enter," she called, wiping away her tears.

Helen appeared in the doorway. "Matthew, yer father needs ye straightaway in the courtyard."

"Thank ye. I will be along shortly."

Helen dipped in a quick curtsy before turning to leave.

Then Matthew, once again, met Cait's gaze. "It would be my pleasure to take yer message to our father...my lady," he said, his eyes shining with pride before he bowed and took his leave.

When she was alone again, Cait took a deep breath and turned back to the window, letting the blanket fall from her shoulders. The cold wind cleared her mind. She breathed deep the crisp air. Closing her eyes, she stood like that for several moments, garnering her strength with every deep breath she took. Finally, she turned away and crossed to her wardrobe and threw open the doors. Her fingers grazed her many tunics. Just as she was reaching for a burgundy wool with deep green trim, trumpets sounded, causing her to jump. Startled, she hastened once more toward the casement.

Campbell warriors had formed two lines on either side of the front gate, extending to the center of the courtyard. Their swords were drawn and ceremoniously raised. Behind them, trumpeters sent a flourish of sound into the air. The courtyard was quickly filling with villagers.

Confused, she leaned out the window, wondering why the sudden fanfare. And then she saw banners flying in the distance. An instant later, riders crested over the hill in formation, with a lone rider in the lead.

Her heart leapt at the sight of golden hair. She covered her mouth with her hand as a fresh sob rose to her lips. Then, she turned and raced from her room. Breathless, she hastened down the stairs and through the great hall. Barreling through the doors that led out to the courtyard, she drew to a halt.

Her family was assembled on the stairs as were Rowan and Lady Alana. Cait crossed to the lady's side and clasped her hand.

"Could it be?" the older woman said, tears streaming down her face.

Cait squeezed her hand and held her breath and shifted her gaze straight on. The trumpeters released another flourish of sound just as the mighty din of pounding hooves reached Cait's ears. Her heart thumped in her chest. Then her breath hitched.

Sitting tall in his saddle, Ewan thundered through the front gates, followed by his men who carried their banners with pride. He drew to a halt. His bearing was strong and his expression resplendent.

"My son," Lady Alana gasped.

Cait's smile could not be contained. Then one of the trumpeters stepped forward. "Welcome, Laird Ewan Patrick Michael MacLeod, the Chieftain of Clan MacLeod!"

Cait sucked in a sharp breath. Her hand covered her mouth against the rush of tears that surged up her throat. Lady Alana dropped to her knees. A choir of cheers erupted throughout the courtyard.

A smile broke across Ewan's face as he slid to the ground, revealing young Timothy behind him. Timothy smiled and waved to the crowd, then swung down and crossed to Ewan's side. Ewan reached out his hand and rested it on Timothy's iron arm. Together, they walked through the line of Campbell warriors and came to stand at the foot of the stairwell.

"I bid ye most welcome, Laird MacLeod," Argyle said, his voice booming.

Ewan dipped his head. "I thank ye, Laird Campbell." Then he squared his shoulders and called out, "Do I have the pleasure of being in the company of the Lady of Castle Shéan?"

Cait opened her mouth to speak but a sob burst from her lips as she raced down the steps and threw herself at Ewan, wrapping her arms around his neck. He stumbled back but caught his footing. His arms came around her, and he lifted her feet off the ground and spun her around. "Ye're here," she cried.

Her toes touched down. Still holding her in his arms, he drew away slightly and pressed his forehead to hers. "I am here," he rasped. "My heart, my name, and my sword are here, and they are all for ye." He cupped her cheeks between his hands. "I love ye, Cait, with all that I am and all I hope to be."

She could not contain her joy. Rising up on her toes, she pressed her lips to his. With a groan, he crushed her against his chest, lifting her feet clear off the ground. He returned her kiss with wild hunger, his lips devouring, his tongue sending shivers of desire coursing through her.

When their lips parted, he vowed, "No more hiding. What say ye, fair Cait?"

She wove her fingers through his thick flaxen hair. "Laird MacLeod, I am so utterly and completely in love with ye."

Ewan threw his head back and whooped to the sky. The next moment, their families descended upon them.

Cait cried anew as Rowan crushed his older brother close. "I'm glad to have ye back."

Waves of emotion passed over Ewan's beautiful features. "I'm glad to be back."

Lady Alana, who was crying tears of pure joy, was pulled into their embrace. Cait watched their happy reunion with a grateful heart.

Before too long, Ewan was at her side again, and soon it was Matthew's turn to pull them both into a fierce hug. "Tonight, we will celebrate the joining of our two families," her brother announced. "It will be the merriest feast Castle Shéan has ever known!"

After they were released from Matthew's bulky arms, Ewan held her close and whispered for her ears alone. "Ye know what this means, don't ye?"

She wrapped her arms around his neck. "What does this mean?"

He smiled. "We're as good as betrothed."

She pressed a kiss to his lips. "Here me, Laird MacLeod," she rasped. "Tomorrow is the first day of Yule. Come the Twelfth Night, we wed, for I do not wish to wait a single day longer to be yer wife."

A sideways smile slowing curved his lips. "Who am I to argue with the lady of the keep?"

Laughter burst from her lips, and he crushed her close. "There is no finer music than yer laughter," he whispered. Then he pulled away and smiled down at her. His fingers lovingly traced the contours of her face. "Mayhap second only to yer piping."

Her heart swelled as he pulled her close once more, and in her mind she heard the song that would drift from her pipe in that moment—the notes, silken and rich, would coil around them in ribbons of light and love, forming a bond that time nor hardship could ever break.

Chapter Nine

Cait looked out the casement of her tall tower. Below her, she glimpsed a line of villagers filing into the chapel. The past twelve days had been the most joyous but also the longest days she had ever known—for her mind had been fixed on her heart's one desire...becoming Ewan's wife, body and soul. Finally, however, Twelfth Night was upon them, and soon she and Ewan would be wed.

As she traced the distant moors with her gaze, she thought for a moment of all the times she had stood in that very spot and looked with longing at a world that had seemed beyond her grasp.

Over the years, so many people had reached through the surface of her pain and bade she take their hand, promising that they could bring her into the light—her father, her brothers, Helen, Arlene, but somehow she never believed it was possible.

Then Ewan walked back into her life, and even though he couldn't see her face, he saw her soul, and within it, he found something she hadn't even known was there—the candle of hope that fate had never truly snuffed out.

Newfound hope had ignited her soul, and suddenly she knew that she had the strength to pull herself free. So, too, did Ewan discover that he had never lost his own strength—not even when fate had stolen his sight.

Now, their wounded souls had healed, and although the scars would always remain—they were two dented pots boiling over with love.

In that moment, her whole body tingled as she thought about the kisses they had stolen in the dark corners of the keep over the last days, and how his hands had roved over her body, awakening a powerful hunger within her that craved satisfaction.

She was boiling all right.

In fact, she was burning hot with desire.

A soft rapping sounded at the door.

She fanned herself to cool her face. "Enter!"

Helen and Arlene filed into the room, their faces beaming with delight. "Look what I finally finished," Helen said as she held up the plum colored tunic with billowing sleeves that had once made Cait so fretful.

Cait laughed as she hastened across the room. "And to think, this fine tunic is to be part of my wedding clothes after all."

Helen chuckled. "Life has a funny way of working out in ways we never dreamed possible."

Arlene dabbed at her eyes with her apron. "I can't believe this day has finally arrived." Then the plump woman shook her head and took a deep breath. "I must stop this carrying on, or else we'll be late to yer own wedding!"

Arlene and Helen set to work helping Cait dress. All the while they both chattered on about the beauty of the kirk, which they said had been decorated with garlands of evergreen and holly.

"And the great hall is magnificent," Helen beamed. "Anna hung bunches of dried flowers from the sconces. The trestle tables have white lace runners, and blue bunting—the very color of yer eyes—has been added to the pine garlands and mistle-toe."

"Now, how should we set yer hair?" Arlene asked, stepping back and giving Cait an appraising look."

"Something ornate but soft—" Helen began, but then Cait interrupted.

"I will wear my hair down and unadorned," she said simply.

Arlene's gaze flashed wide. "Nay, my lady. Ye must wear a veil in the least."

"I will cover my head just while we are in the chapel."

"But, 'tis yer wedding day, my lady," Helen said, her voice beseeching.

"And my husband-to-be prefers the feel of my hair down," Cait said pointedly.

Arlene's cheeks pinkened. "Oh my," she said breathlessly.

"Well, in that case," Helen said with a glint in her eye. "We shall brush it out until it flows like a river down yer back."

Before too long, Cait stood in front of her womenfolk as they assessed her appearance.

"Ye look beautiful, my lady," Helen said at last.

Arlene's round cheeks turned crimson as she blurted, "And ye feel beautiful, too!"

Their giggles echoed down the stairwell as they descended toward the great hall where Cait met her father who was awaiting her arrival. When he saw her, his eyes flooded with tears.

Helen cleared her throat and bobbed in a quick curtsy. "We shall take our leave and make our way to the chapel."

When they were alone, her father pulled her into a warm embrace. "Ye do my heart proud," he said. Then he cleared his throat. "Come along and let us not speak or else I will arrive at the kirk a blubbering mess."

She threw her arms around his neck. "Thank ye, Da," she whispered.

"Thank ye for being the bravest and the kindest daughter a father has ever—" His voice broke. "Blast it all!" he said, as his tears streamed into his bushy black beard. Then he lifted his shoulders. "There's no shame in a man crying, especially on his daughter's wedding day."

Cait smiled through her tears. "None at all."

On her father's arm, Cait walked to the chapel, all the while her heart pounded in her chest. And when, at last, they stepped into the nave, she drank in the sight of Ewan standing at the altar with Rowan at his side. Her gaze took in the breadth of his strong shoulders and lean, muscular physique. But as she started down the aisle on her father's arm, Ewan's head remained bowed, his stance unchanged. A moment later, Timothy darted up the altar steps and whispered in Ewan's ear. Ewan straightened. Smiling, his sightless gaze darted about the room. Then Timothy turned about, and her gaze locked with his.

"Thank ye," she mouthed to the young lad. He smiled and dipped his head to her before, retreating to his place among the villagers.

Now, anticipation filled Ewan's bearing. And when, at last, their hands joined, a surge of emotion shot through her. Her breath caught. For in that moment, their souls came together, and she knew that they would never again be apart.

EWAN STOOD AT THE BASE of the stairs that led to Cait's chamber tower. His heart raced as he paced back and forth, switching hands so that he never lost contact with the wall.

When a choir of giggles reached his ears, he froze.

"Good eventide, Laird MacLeod," a woman's voice said. "'Tis I, Helen." She cleared her throat. "We have a message from our lady."

A new woman chimed in. "She will signal to ye when she is ready," the woman said. "Oh, by the by, 'tis I, Arlene."

Ewan smiled. "Thank ye, Helen. And, Arlene, please accept my gratitude. Tonight's supper was magnificent."

A fresh round of giggles met his ears.

"Thank ye, Laird MacLeod," Arlene replied. "Good eventide!"

He listened while their footfalls hastened down the corridor. Then he turned back to the stairwell and sat down on the first step. Resting his head against the wall, he closed his eyes. An image came to his mind of unbound black waves and limpid blue eyes. His hands ached to hold his wife.

"My wife," he whispered aloud, savoring the words.

And then, a faint sound rose above the din of his pounding heart. A smile curved his lips as a sensuous melody flowed down to him, beckoning him to come to her. His body hard with desire, he circled the steps, taking them two at a time.

He threw open her door. "Set down yer pipe," he rasped as he closed the door behind him. "Because I am about to caress every inch of yer body."

He crossed the room, to the bed, and reached down. His hand grazed supple, bare skin.

"I am ready," she rasped.

His heart racing, his fingers trailed down her long neck, her skin soft and bare to his touch. His fingers continued their journey, meeting only silken skin. He groaned, realizing she was naked. Slowly, his hand cupped her full breast.

A soft moan escaped her lips. Straightening, he freed himself from the constraints of his own clothing before he sank onto the bed beside her. His mouth claimed hers with a hunger he had never known. His tongue traced the soft fullness of her lips. With a gasp, her lips parted. He plunged his tongue into the recesses of her mouth, tasting, teasing. She returned his kiss with a hunger all her own, her hands weaving through his hair, demanding, wanting.

Tearing his lips free, his tongue continued to explore the soft skin of her neck and shoulders while his hands curved over her breasts. His thumb grazed her taut nipple. With a hungry growl, he pulled one of the hard peaks into his mouth. Tasting, teasing, first one, then the other. Her gasps of pleasure served to fuel his own passion to new heights as his hand coursed over the smooth skin of her sumptuous hips and soft thighs. Stroking, caressing, he explored her gentle curves, until he found the heat of her womanhood at the apex of her full thighs. She parted her legs, pressing into his touch.

A hungry moan fled her lips. "Ewan," she breathed, her tone pleading. "Make me yers!"

"Not yet," he rasped. "Remember, I said every inch of yer body." He shifted between her legs, bringing his lips first to the tender skin of her thighs, then slowly, closer and closer until, at last, he tasted her honeyed warmth. She trembled beneath his touch, her soft moans building, first soft, desperate with want, then becoming louder and louder.

"Please," she cried out.

His body, hard and hungry, ached to fill her. He could wait no longer. Moving over her, he steeled his shoulders to ensure he did not enter her tight sheath too swiftly. Slowly, he eased his hard length inside her. Her nails dug into his back as she stiffened. He strained to hold still until her body softened around him. Then, she melted in his arms, her legs circling his waist. He thrust deep inside her, then deeper still. Her breaths came in great heaves. She clung to him, fully surrendering to the passion that moved through his own body like wildfire. A tremor shuddered through her, her body tightening around his hard length. Then, she cried out, pushing his own need beyond his control as he thrust again and again, yielding to the searing hunger that pushed him higher and higher; until he cried out as waves of ecstasy coursed through him.

Breathless, they clung to each other, their hearts pounding in fierce unity.

When he, at last, caught his breath, he moved to her side and pulled her close. His body curved around hers, but then he stiffened, feeling her tremble in his arms.

"Cait, are ye all right?"

"All right?" she repeated. "What I feel goes far beyond all right." She shifted in his arms and cupped his cheek. "I don't even feel dented anymore. I feel full and sumptuous and perfect."

A smile curved his lips as he stroked his hand over her supple hips. "Ye are perfect, just as ye are."

"As are ye."

Her softly spoken words made his heart swell. "I love ye, Cait MacLeod, Lady of Castle Laoch." He kissed her tenderly. Then, their lips parted. "Are ye ready?" he rasped.

"To be Lady of Castle Laoch?" she asked.

"That we already know beyond a doubt. My hunger for ye, on the other hand, has not yet been sated." He tickled her playfully. Her laughter rang out, and he knew then that even the beauty of her piping could never compare to the sound of her happiness.

"Come to me, my golden knight," she rasped. "Make me whole again."

"Forever mine, forever yers, forever whole," he vowed. Then, his lips claimed hers as he kissed her with all the love beating inside his full heart.

Thank you for reading *The Piper*. What's next?

Keep reading to find out!

The Tempest releases on August 9ᵗʰ 2022.
Now available for Pre-Order

★★★★★ *"Lily Baldwin books are full of tension and desire. One of my favorite authors." ~ Kindle Customer*

The harder they try to stay apart, the more fate traps them together.

Lady Tempest Brodie is reckless and impulsive. She always does exactly as she pleases whether that be taming wild horses or falling in love with the quiet, yet compelling stranger sleeping in the loft above the castle stables. But what if he is not the man she believes him to be? What if he is secretly dangerous and shamelessly savage?

Caleb is the nameless son of no one, a bounty hunter with a past who never loses control and has a preference for solitude. He has promised the lady and laird of Castle Bron to protect Tempest while they are away; that is, until he realizes the greatest threat to her safety...is himself.

More by Lily Baldwin...

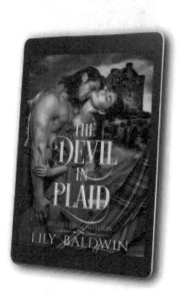

★★★★★ *"Absolutely must read!"*

★★★★★ *"Beautifully written and vividly imagined..."*

★★★★★ *"Masterfully written story!"*

A passion too intense to deny...

Lady Fiona MacDonnell is certain Laird Jamie MacLeod is the devil himself. Their clans are sworn enemies, each steeped in hatred born from a long-standing feud. But when threatened by a powerful neighboring clan, they must unite to survive.

The Devil has never been hotter, his angel never so fine, but will their forced marriage be hell on Earth or together will they find heaven?

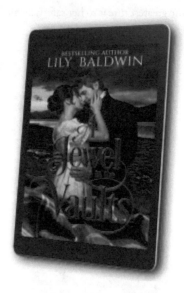

★★★★★ *"A Powerful story of survival and love."*

★★★★★ *"This book will tug at your heart and bring tears to your eyes."*

In 1802, Edinburgh's poverty-ridden Old Town is rife with danger, but it is the only home Robbie MacKenzie has ever known. To safeguard herself against the worst villains of the street, Robbie conceals her femininity behind her shorn hair, dirt-smeared face, and tattered breeches. To all the world she is a lad, but beneath the ruse is a woman aching to break free.

Leaving his beloved Highlands behind in pursuit of his prodigal brother, Conall MacKay journeys to Edinburgh. There, he solicits the aid of a young street lad named Robbie. But Conall soon realizes that there is more to both Robbie and Edinburgh's Old Town than meets the eye.

In a world where wickedness governs and darkness reigns, a savage struggle for dignity, survival, and love begins.

Keep reading to enjoy a sample of A Jewel in the Vaults...

Prologue
Paris, France
June 1782

"*Hell is empty, and all the devils are here.*" ~ *William Shakespeare, The Tempest*

"*Au revoir, salut,*" Claudine Doucet said to her fellow actors as she exited the stage and made her way to the back entrance of the Théâtre du Marcais. Her farewell was met with disapproval as the revelers on stage pleaded with her to stay.

Luc peered around the curtain. "*Ma chérie*, tonight was your night. All of Paris drinks to you. Why must you leave? It is not yet morning."

She hated to disappoint everyone, especially Luc who was the first friend she had made upon her arrival alone in Paris three years before.

"I am tired, Luc. I wish to stay, but I must rest," Claudine said as she pressed a kiss to his cheek and bid him goodnight once more.

She flung open the door and felt the rush of night air on her neck as she stepped onto the Rue de Tourigny. An irrepressible noise akin to a squeal escaped her lips as she flung her neck back and stretched her arms toward the diamond-studded sky. Decorum and the bone stays compressing her torso restricted her display of excitement, but despite outer appearances, waves of exhilaration coursed through her, chasing away her fatigue.

She had been born the daughter of a clerk in a small provincial town. Three years ago, on the eve of her fifteenth birthday, her father had knelt on the ground near her mattress and brushed a wayward lock of golden hair from her face. Then he told her that God did not make such a beauty as she to remain cloistered among the trees and fields.

"*Mon enfant*," he had said, his eyes wet with tears. "You must go and make your way in this world, for there is nothing here for you. Let Paris witness your beauty. Fall in love. You are fated for happiness—this I do not doubt, *mon bijou.*" *My jewel.*

How she wished her papa could have been in the audience that night. She closed her eyes against the ache which pushed to the fore of her emotions. She had been in Paris not even a month when she received word of his death.

"*Merci*, Papa," she whispered as silent tears coursed down her cheeks. The glory of the evening returned to her, and she relived her debut performance in her mind. When the curtain fell after the final call, she had sunk to her knees and sobbed while applause still thundered from the audience. She had swum in a sea of flowers cast by admirers upon the stage. The dreams of youth had become her reality, and this realization made her heart quake.

She scanned the narrow cobbled streets rife with pedestrians and carriages. It was the strange hour where night and morning collide. Some of the passersby were dragging their tired bodies home after a long night of work. Others, more fortunate souls, were clad as she in fine silks, and were returning home after an evening spent enjoying the pleasures and excesses permitted their station in life. For many, their day had just begun as they tarried with wagons and baskets of goods or were rushing to take up their places in one of the factories. She glimpsed some rag pickers going through the streets looking for scraps of metal, glass, fabric—anything that might fetch a price. Greasy bags hung from their shoulders. They were frail, and hunger flooded their eyes with desperate yearning. She grimaced as she turned away, muttering a prayer of gratitude for her blessings. Her hands smoothed her sapphire blue silk gown over her ruffled petticoat before she stepped toward the coach that waited to bring her to her apartment.

"*Bonjour, Mademoiselle.*"

Claudine whirled around to see a tall man step from the shadows into the soft light of the streetlamp. His dark eyes, filled with soft warmth, instantly entreated her trust. She felt at ease despite his being a stranger.

"*Pardonnez-moi, Mademoiselle*, but do you speak English?" he asked. His deep voice surrounded her. She puzzled over his accent.

"*Oui, Monsieur*. A little. But you do not sound English."

"And for good reason. I am Scottish, lass, and you are lovely," he said before taking her hand. Then he pulled her yellow glove down, sliding the silk off her fingers. His lips grazed her palm, sending currents of warmth drifting through her body.

Bowing over her hand, he said, "My name is Lord James MacKenzie." He glanced up at her. "You were magnificent tonight," he whispered.

Lord James MacKenzie was tall and grand, dressed impeccably in a rich velvet coat fitted to his broad shoulders, but it was not his fine attire or obvious wealth that led Claudine to accept his offered arm. His eyes laid his soul bare to her, and she lost herself to the possibility of love she glimpsed in their sterling depths.

Night began its slow retreat while Claudine and James walked along the river Seine. From Pont Neuf they welcomed the new dawn. The cobbles glimmered as the dusky shades of light caught the fine mist, which bathed the roads and bridges.

In the weeks that followed, it became their practice. James would wait for Claudine every night by the theater's back entrance, and they would stroll the cobbled streets of Paris until the sun rose and the need for sleep could no longer be denied. With words of love on his lips, it was not long before Claudine welcomed James into her bed, and from that moment on, she belonged to him.

Edinburgh, Scotland
February 1784

"PLEASE, I NEED A BED. *S'il vous plaît, Madame.* I am with child, and my time draws near. Please, take pity on us," Claudine pleaded, cradling her round belly. "I do not ask for charity. I can pay." The owner of the common lodging-house, Molly, who was a handsome woman with red hair piled on top of her head, seemed to consider the coin in Claudine's outstretched palm.

"Please, *Madame.*" A knot comprised of dread and hope filled Claudine's throat as she looked up at the woman who with a simple aye or nay could decide the future of Claudine and her unborn child.

Molly shook her head. "Nay, lass. I cannae let ye in and ye ken why. The lady whose husband gave ye that babe has forbidden it. Lady MacKenzie is a right bitch. I will not invite her vengeance, not even for a sweet lass like yourself. Find your way home, Claudine Doucet. Ye will not find a bed in Edinburgh, nor will ye find any honest work." Molly's face softened. "In a few years, when the haughty cow has forgotten all about ye, then I will give ye a bed."

Despair drained the last hope from her soul as Molly slowly eased the door shut. The wind picked up, whistling down the alley. Her arms encircled her swollen stomach, shielding her baby from the fierce cold. Black soot covered the stone buildings that lined the narrow street on both sides, making the night appear even darker. Only a strip of starless sky could she see above the rooftops that were six and seven stories high. If she could climb to stand above the filth of the surrounding slums, could she reach her arms toward heaven? And if she could, would the good Lord above save her, or would he, too, fear the wrath of Lady Eleanor MacKenzie?

Snow appeared in the air, drifting through the light of the one lamp that set aglow the far end of the street. She pulled her tattered shawl tighter about her shoulders and scrambled around the side of a nearby stairwell, seeking shelter from the snow, but as she peered beneath the stoop, a huddled mass of ragged children growled up at her, baring their teeth like feral creatures.

She turned and ran, fleeing the alley, wishing she could flee from the world. Tears choked her breath as she sobbed her misery to the sky. There was no more hope; she had sinned too grievously. She had been foolish to try to possess that which could never be hers. Upon their arrival in Edinburgh, James had confessed that he was, indeed, a married man. She should have turned away from him then and there. She should have cursed his lies, his promises, but love had bidden her stay by his side.

Now, she raced down the street, slipping and stumbling upon the snowy cobbles. She turned onto Cowgate, a street that three months ago she would not have dared to walk down, even in the light of day. The crowded street forced her to slow her pace. She eyed the women she passed with their torn, faded gowns, their dirt-smeared faces, and hungry eyes. And then she froze and looked down at her roughened fingers and the greasy sway of her own threadbare skirt in the icy breeze. She gaped at the surrounding despair and realized the slums mirrored her own pain, her own unhappy end.

When the Lady MacKenzie had discovered her husband's affair, she had forced James to cast her aside, but it had not ended there. His wife had not been satisfied until she had brought about the ruination of Claudine Doucet. Lady Eleanor had ensured Claudine was barred from every theater. She could not even find work as a seamstress. No inn or lodging house would take her. She was nothing now but one of countless souls who passed each night wondering if they would have to face the dawn or if hunger or cold would at last bring them peace.

"Aren't ye a pretty bit of skirt," an old woman said as she shuffled toward Claudine. Claudine eyed the woman warily. Her stooped shoulders were covered with the remnants of a ragged jacket. Creases lined her face, but her eyes were sharp and unwavering. "Ye need a bed, love?"

Claudine nodded and dropped the last of her coin in the woman's outstretched hand. Then Claudine followed her inside a nearby door, which opened to a stairway that descended into darkness. The old woman clasped tightly to Claudine's fingers, leading her through unknown spaces devoid of light.

"Where do you take me?" Claudine asked, though she feared the answer.

"These are the vaults, dearie, tunnels and chambers built into the bridges. 'Tis dark and foul, but the snow cannae reach ye down here."

Claudine felt the crushing weight of the city above. Thick, fetid air surrounded them, consuming what little joy she still possessed.

"Here, lass," the old woman said as she pulled Claudine into a cramped space. Claudine felt what her eyes could not see. It appeared to be a shelf with just enough room to lie down. "Ye shall rest here and let ol' Peggy care for ye."

Claudine surrendered to Peggy's comfort and laid down upon her stone bed. Steeped in darkness, she fell asleep to the moans and wails of others who slept entombed beneath the city.

That night, she dreamt of glittering light and lilting laughter, softness, and perfumed breezes. She felt full and content, swathed in silk with the taste of champagne on her tongue. But then a stirring in her abdomen pulled her from the sweetness of her dreams.

"*Mon Dieu*," she cried as her womb cramped and pain shot through her back.

Sweat dampened her brow. It seemed the walls were closing in on her, smothering her breath.

"There, there, lass," Peggy said, suddenly at her side. "Do not panic. 'Twill be done soon."

"*Non, non*," Claudine screamed. "Please, I cannot give birth to my child down here in this hell."

"Hush now, lass. Save your strength. It makes little difference whether your child draws its first breath here or up on the streets. Either way the air is foul."

Claudine gripped her abdomen as another pain twisted inside of her. "Either way my baby is damned," she whispered. "Just as I am damned."

Hours of toil passed when at last her baby's first cry echoed through the tunnels.

"She is strong," Peggy exclaimed. "Listen to her cry."

Claudine strained in the darkness to see the face of her newborn babe, but she could not. "*Oui*, he is a strong boy," Claudine cooed as she pressed kisses to her baby's cheeks.

"Nay, Claudine. 'Tis a lass. Feel for yourself. Ye have a daughter."

"Listen to me, Peggy. Had I a daughter I would show her the mercy God has refused me, and I would slit her throat right here and end her suffering. The slums would feast on her and make her a whore before her body even had time to ripen. This child is a boy. Do you understand, Peggy? His name is Robbie, Robbie MacKenzie. And he will rise from this hell." She held her child to her bosom, and whispered, "Robbie, you must fight. Fight to breathe. Fight to live. You are fated for happiness—this I do not doubt, *mon bijou*." *My jewel.*

Scotland 1802

The might of the Highland wind struggled to compel Conall MacKay back from whence he had come. It whipped his long hair into a frenzy, obscuring the path before him and tempted his senses with the perfume of the sea and the heady scent of the damp earth. Still, he fought against the wind's power and kept his southerly course, a course that would lead him away from the Highlands and everything good and green, toward land now marked by the black stain of industry and greed.

Too soon, the earth around him began to change. Rugged, wild moors, carved into pieces by jutting rocks, gave way to smooth fields and bustling villages. It was the land he had once described to his Aunt Agnes, who never strayed but a mile or two from home, as being tame. He shook his head in disgust as mining posts and iron mills rose up before him. This land was no longer tame. It was beaten.

The wind could not follow. Billowing black clouds of soot and smoke wrapped their fingers around the currents of clean air, smothering its magic. His hair now lay unmoving down his back. The wind had retreated. He would go on alone without the rush of air from the sea or the familiar scents of home.

For at least the tenth time that hour, Conall cursed his younger brother, Davis, for having left Cape Wrath in the first place. Conall would never understand his brother's desire to flee their home on the north westerly tip of the Scottish mainland. He closed his eyes for a moment and pictured the rocky hills that gradually sloped down to the coast where beaches of white sand shone in the sun. Further down the coast, cliffs rose up from the waves, towering above the water.

His croft was nestled in a small valley between two steep bluffs. From the south, his house was hidden by the hills, but to the north, his land stretched out until a narrow cliff marked its abrupt end. In the evening, it was his practice to watch the sunset. He would leave his door and walk straight until his toes teetered on the edge of the cliff, and then he would wait patiently for the spectacle to begin. As the day drew to a close, the world would be dipped in gold and coated with jewels of light cast by the sun's glow. He could not summon dreams of greater treasure or beauty than what awaited him just outside his door; however, the same could not be said of Davis.

Davis gathered impossible dreams like cherished keepsakes. He rejected the quiet beauty of the land to which he belonged and hungered instead for material abundance. Conall reminded Davis that such riches were possessed by only a few who lorded their wealth over many, but Davis would not be swayed. The life of a farmer was no life at all, he would say. Much to Conall's dismay, Davis longed to trade the towering cliffs and storm-tossed seas of Cape Wrath for the stone buildings and bridges of Edinburgh, dirt roads for cobbled streets, space and air for the crowded and tainted. Only in a city where excess and depravity ruled could Davis have his heart's desire: money, fine suits, cigars, and, of course, women.

Conall's taste ran much simpler. Nothing pleased him more than the feel of cool earth sifting between his fingers or the satisfaction of a successful harvest. His croft was one of twenty on Cape Wrath, all home to families tied to the land, their devotion as steadfast as the cliffs themselves. Most could trace their lineage back to the days of the chieftains when the MacKay territory spanned out for miles.

Conall seldom considered the world beyond his croft. He traveled from his home fashioned of stone and thatch only when demand called him away, although it had not always been thus. Long ago, it seemed to him now, he had been married. When his wife, Mary, still lived, they would frequent the near-by village of Durness, but illness stole his young bride when he was not yet nineteen. Heartbroken, he gave his grief to the land and withdrew from village life. Now at twenty-six, he made peace with love lost and the resulting solitude. Unlike Davis, his life was a collection of simple pleasures and humble dreams. Conall tried his best to quell Davis's baser inclinations with lessons in swordplay, animal husbandry, and fishing, but Davis merely scoffed at such honest pursuits. He craved excitement and always had. Several months ago, he had left Cape Wrath behind determined to join a Scottish regiment, or so he had claimed.

Two days ago, Conall was paid a visit by Gordon MacKay who resided in the village. He had encountered Davis in Edinburgh during a brief stay on his return from London, and his report was ill, indeed. He remarked on Davis's lack of Scottish regimentals. Not only did Davis not appear to be a soldier, but judging by his mixed company, Gordon suspected Davis had found little other than trouble in Edinburgh. What worried Conall most was Gordon's account that Davis had appeared frail and strangely agitated when Gordon had approached him. Only a few words were exchanged when Davis made excuses to leave, heading toward Cowgate, the lowliest part of the city.

As much as Conall wished to make light of Gordon's report, the love he bore his brother would not be silenced. Davis had never been anything but trouble since he was a wee lad, but despite his follies, he had a kind and trusting nature. Besides, he was blood, and Conall was raised to honor blood ties above all others.

The irritating clacking of his horse's hooves on the cobbled roads filled Conall's ears as he rode toward Edinburgh. While still on the outskirts of the city, he closed his eyes and inhaled deeply. He searched the slight breeze for just a taste of the Highlands, but only the acrid scents of city life hung in the air.

He left his horse at the livery stable near St James's Square in the New Town and then walked the short distance to a narrow street where he hoped the Cummings Inn would have a room available. In the past five years, the business of settling first his parent's accounts when they passed away and later his uncle's had compelled him to visit Edinburgh. On both occasions he stayed at the same quiet inn. He knew he could count on Mrs. Cummings running a clean and respectable business. Her fine cooking and one of her comfortable rooms were crucial to maintaining his sanity while in the midst of Edinburgh's noise and congestion.

It was early in the evening when he arrived at the inn. After a fine dinner, he thanked Mrs. Cummings and left the comforts of the inn behind. He knew where he had to go, Cowgate, but before he could face the inhumane conditions of Edinburgh's Old Town, he first needed a guide—someone who knew the streets and would not raise immediate suspicion. A stranger could not enter Cowgate and expect a warm reception, especially a Highlander. He pushed aside the sudden voice in his head that warned all was for naught. Desperation and corruption strangled all hope from that dark street. Davis's knavish appetites would attract the most crooked and unscrupulous villains that Cowgate had to offer. Conall prayed that he might find Davis before misfortune did.

Clinging to hope, he made his way to Prince's Street. Affluence gleamed from every brick stacked with care to form the townhouses and shops, which served the wealthiest of Edinburgh's citizens. Men in knee breeches with silk stockings, fine waistcoats, and top hats moved with leisure down the wide, clean cobbled street. Through narrow lids, they assessed everyone they passed with a haughty air of dominance. These were men used to their own way who served only themselves. Conall wished nothing more than to punch the smug expression from each of their faces.

On the other hand, the women seemed to move without a care. They lacked the strength and presence of Highland women. Like pretty snowflakes, they fluttered about in dresses of varying shades of white, some plain or embroidered with flowers, but otherwise they all looked the same. The dresses fell straight, close to their figures and cinched not at the waist but beneath their bosoms. Lace trimmings, attached at the low necklines, provided at least some modesty. In his mind, he could hear his Aunt Agnes tsking her disapproval.

The empire waist gowns were worn in his village as well, but they were made of sturdier fabrics. Although it was late spring, there was a chill in the evening air. Still, none of the lasses wore cloaks or jackets. He had to resist the urge to throw a shawl or blanket around a young woman's shoulders who could not have been much older than thirteen. He held his tongue as he hurried passed, but much to his amusement, the lass, who gasped when she saw him, was not as capable as he at concealing her thoughts. He earned similar responses from four young women walking in his direction who suddenly stopped when they saw the large Highlander in their path. He almost laughed out loud when they hurried to cross the street, nearly tripping over themselves in their haste to keep their distance. He pretended not to notice as he turned on to St. David's Street. Accustomed to the flurry of interest he incited upon entering Scotland's southern cities, he was not at all surprised that he was quickly becoming the center of attention. To the typical lowlander, he was an uncommon sight.

At nearly six and a half feet in height he towered over most men. Current fashion demanded men trim their hair short around the ears and at the nape. His light brown hair fell free down his back. His legs were not burdened by breeches, nor did he carry a cane. He wore a kilt, belted at his hips, a linen shirt, and a plain wool jacket. Wool socks were folded at the knee and ended in a pair of deer hide shoes. His sporran completed his attire. He looked as foreign in his own country as he might in one of the distant colonies. He stopped to allow the passing of several carriages, the occupants of which all stared at him, the ladies hiding their interest behind their fans.

The stares of onlookers were forgotten as he crossed to the other side of the street, for someone had caught his attention, someone who appeared to belong in that place even less than he. A boy of no more than thirteen or fourteen years was slumped against a building, shielded by a fine carriage whose footman was occupied speaking with the proprietor of a dress shop. The boy stood out among the manicured trees and bushes and polished inhabitants of Edinburgh's New Town with his bruised and dirt-smeared face, but no one seemed to note his presence, except for Conall. The lad's quick darting eyes conveyed his dishonest intent. The young urchin was just the sort of person who might aid Conall on his quest to locate his brother.

He started toward the lad but then froze when the small, ragged body slunk back against the wall and held so still that he appeared to vanish into shadow. Meanwhile, two gentlemen passed by his hiding place. Conall noted with amusement that the pompous men noticed the lad no more than they would a smudge on the cobbles. And then something incredible happened. Conall could scarce believe his own eyes. The lad's hand flashed out of his filth covered jacket, and with a touch, which must have been as soft as a sea breeze, he pinched a bag of coin from inside the nearest gentleman's jacket. No sooner did the lad grab the purse than he dashed away and turned off down Thistle Street.

With a grin Conall followed. His long stride overtook the lad whom he grabbed by the back of the jacket and lifted into the air. "I am willing to bet ye thought ye'd made a fine escape," Conall said, smiling.

A Jewel in the Vaults is available in ebook and paperback. Thank you again for reading The Piper. Wishing you happy reading and many blessings.
All my best,
Lily

Made in United States
Troutdale, OR
09/28/2023